My Claustro
Happiness

Copyright © 2020 Jeanne Randolph

ARP Books (Arbeiter Ring Publishing)
205-70 Arthur Street
Winnipeg, Manitoba
Treaty 1 Territory and Historic Métis Nation Homeland
Canada R3B 1G7
arpbooks.org

Book design and layout by LOKI.
Printed and bound in Canada by Imprimerie Gauvin on paper made from 100% recycled post-consumer waste.

COPYRIGHT NOTICE
This book is fully protected under the copyright laws of Canada and all other countries of the Copyright Union and is subject to royalty.

ARP Books acknowledges the generous support of the Manitoba Arts Council and the Canada Council for the Arts for our publishing program. We acknowledge the financial support of the Government of Canada and the Province of Manitoba through the Book Publishing Tax Credit and the Book Publisher Marketing Assistance Program of Manitoba Culture, Heritage, and Tourism.

LIBRARY AND ARCHIVES CANADA CATALOGUING IN PUBLICATION
Title: My claustrophobic happiness / Jeanne Randolph.
Names: Randolph, Jeanne, 1943- author.
Identifiers: Canadiana (print) 20200302310 |
Canadiana (ebook) 20200302388 |
ISBN 9781927886410 (softcover) |
ISBN 9781927886427 (ebook)
Classification: LCC PS8585.A5456 M92 2020 | DDC C813/.54—dc23

MY CLAUSTRO PHOBIC HAPPI NESS

Jeanne Randolph

ARP BOOKS · WINNIPEG MB

CONTENTS

TINY LINEN RECTANGLE 10
FRENCH FOREST 13
THE HIT MAN 16
SILVER PINK 19
A ROOM WITH BLUE BEDSPREADS 22
THE MOST BEAUTIFUL DRESS IN THE WORLD 25
QUEEN ELIZABETH II 28
SLICE OF EARTH 31
UGLY DAVID 34
THE JESTER 37
TEMPTATION IN THE DESERT 40
BLACK TREASURE 44
GHOST 47
THE BARBER OF MEADOWLAKE 50
STONE AND COIL 53
DOWN IN THE MINES 56
HEAD 59
ATHLETE WITH BARBELL 62
J'ADORE 65
SNOWY LANE 68
ISHTAR 71
GREEN MAN 74
SHIKAAKWA 77
PRINCE AND PRINCESS 80
FEDORA 83
UNABRIDGED 86
FEU D'ARTIFICE 89
UNDER THE CHANDELIER 92

*L*ike so many of us La Betty had been inculcated with the notion that gold is precious. La Betty had readily observed that gold bestows its majesty upon a wealth of useful as well as superfluous products.

La Betty was especially charmed by gold leaf. Almost intangible, divinely flat, gold leaf was a marvel to La Betty. She loved gold lettering on pebbled glass, the metallic bubbles of Danziger Goldwasser, the calm chill of Cleopatra Gold facial sheets, dainty 24 karat champagne Jell-O cubes, delectable gold-polka-dot chocolate truffles.

One evening La Betty tried to wish herself into a gold chrysalis. La Betty believed that the happiest butterfly in the world is the oleander butterfly — because its chrysalis is gold. And the silver air holes atop the oleander butterfly's chrysalis are serenely ornamental. Gold, she thought, inspires other butterflies. La Betty clothed herself in her antique green silk Fortuny dressing gown, white silk stockings and her baby harp seal fur slippers. La Betty anticipated ecstasy.

La Betty stood in the middle of the living room as if she had just alighted on a pink oleander blossom. In La Betty's version of metamorphosis the ethereal butterfly glides directly into its golden pod. La Betty wouldn't disgust herself thinking of caterpillars and eggs.

Soon La Betty felt ensconced in a golden chrysalis. If only this could be her world. Her condo walls would move closer and closer to her chrysalis. So enchanting is the power of gold that the condo walls would dissolve into it. All furnishings and ornaments would go flat as gold leaf, and then be absorbed.

A gilded constriction began. The constriction continued inexorably, but La Betty's highly volumized hair could not fit into the chrysalis. La Betty's blond hair bunched up in a curly mess. It flopped out the top of the chrysalis and blocked the air holes. La Betty began to gasp. She couldn't wiggle or inhale deeply. La Betty was immobilized. Errant strands of blond hair were in La Betty's mouth, her arms were bound at her side, her rings grinding into her fingers, her silk gown hiking up above her knees. What little air was left in the chrysalis smelled like cheap aftershave.

As the chrysalis continued to suffocate La Betty, she realized the truth of her predicament. La Betty was in the grips of a perverse interruption. A hostile entity had taken her in its golden grasp. A conniving imp was masquerading as the gold chrysalis. It was restraining La Betty like a bewitched girdle. The fake chrysalis kept pinching La Betty all over, and claustrophobia began to squeeze her even more. This phantasm's intention was to torment La Betty till she embraced whatever despicable conviction it upheld. The fiend was set to attain its perverse ambition. It was tempting LaBetty into masochism, squeezing her, forcing an unprecedented sensation, pressing an inescapable metamorphosis:

> "Obsessions are worth attendant annoyances and trouble. The annoyances and trouble become familiar. You find yourself accepting these pains. Next you anticipate them. Eventually when you anticipate them you will not cringe. You will begin to welcome them as inherent to your obsession. Finally you crave them:
>
> you have developed a masochistic disposition. Forever more you can enjoy both your obsession and the pain! A person who enjoys pain is more fit for the human condition than one who avoids it."

Instantly La Betty gloated. The false chrysalis had stupidly miscalculated the basic fact of pain—it ignites awareness of the body.

La Betty's body was fictional, and La Betty had set her lifestyle permanently on the plane of Spectacle. La Betty's flat shimmering vision of life was virtually Byzantine. The gold backdrop of unnatural Byzantine saints matched La Betty's ethos perfectly. La Betty owned absolutely everything necessary to adore images a thousand times more than time or space.

La Betty mocked the masochistic imp: "Kinky-Curly Curling Custard: This volumizing gel is sure to boost your blow-dry! Boost your blow dry! Boost your blow dry!" Not La Betty's defiance, but La Betty's massive gyrating coiffure shattered the chrysalis, which sprinkled to the floor in a zillion specks of golden glitter.

La Betty began to breathe triumphantly. Each inhalation was as fresh as a Norwegian zephyr. La Betty was eager to celebrate with a spontaneous oration. She wanted to sing. But all La Betty could think of were ingredients for the most expensive bath in the world,

> *Me Bath*, with 100% certified
> Hawaiian deep-sea water,
> enriched with rare Sidr honey,
> hand-harvested Peruvian pink salt,
> rich illipe, murumuru
> and kokum butters,
> Israeli jojoba oil,
> and 24-carat gold.

Tiny Linen Rectangle

Remembering the touch of her mother's hand La Betty cringed. Not that her mother's mothering was eerie. Since babyhood La Betty had increasingly considered any creature's living skin to be eerie. As a child La Betty had studied her own skin—hands, legs, belly—and had been nauseated.

At the age of twenty-two La Betty's haphephobia was amplified when she unexpectedly noticed a PBS documentary presenting an outline of evolution. From that moment La Betty was certain every organ of the human body had begun as a distinct colony of aquatic animalcules that long ago were swallowed, but not digested, by a huge swimming bag of living skin. La Betty decided not to ever again expose her mind, soul or body, not even for a moment, to biology, embryology, physiology, anatomy, pathology and certainly not dermatology.

By age twenty-four La Betty had spent her entire cash inheritance on a condo overlooking English Bay. She could stare out the window without seeing people. La Betty's trust fund was forever and so La Betty had easily secured every possible furnishing and service necessary to maintain her health, her beauty and her attention to iPhone, iPad, laptop, TV, even a radio. In this perfect prison of financial freedom La Betty shielded her soul from every reminder of organic humanity, especially her own.

La Betty then persuaded herself that everything, even when it appears most solid, is, in its finality, only a thought, a mirage presented by the brain. Most importantly, thought does not have a skin. This disembodied view led La Betty to adore mass media advertising. And advertising led her to adore shopping. A really effective image would impel La Betty to make a purchase. Yet La Betty's was not compulsive shopping; it was compulsive attention to the possibility of shopping. As a shopping adept, eschewing analysis or fact, La Betty restricted her acquisitive desire to objects favoured by celebrity endorsement and a breath-taking price. These criteria confirmed, La Betty knew what she liked. It is probably accurate to say consumerism replaced her insanity.

One day an antique green silk Fortuny dressing gown had arrived by amazon.com drone. The elegant undulating gown was embroidered with gold curlicues aligned in parallel from décolletage to hem. Tightly coiled, the dainty glittering curlicues were almost but not quite rosebuds. Dozens of silk acanthus appliqués complemented the curlicues.

La Betty was always curious to inspect a garment's label. This one was an ornately detailed quite tiny linen rectangle, upon which a finely embroidered design was perceptible. As if brushstrokes, each delicate thread was mimicking the style of a seventeenth century oil painting in a tortuously carved dark walnut frame. Inevitably La Betty perceived the label as an actual screen far teensier than her iPhone screen. Soon, framed by darkness, an image of a comely young Dutch woman became visible. Portrayed in pliant thread the woman was breathing and shifting. La Betty shuddered at the woman's supple cheeriness, and La Betty was agog at the woman's bosom. The expanse of voluptuous flesh catapulted La Betty into a panic.

La Betty gasped. She knew immediately of course that this image had been deliberately conjured to arouse the senses. There had to be an uncouth entity, a wraith somewhere in the room, something jeering at La Betty's lifestyle, polluting the chaste superficiality of La Betty's expensive tastes.

La Betty fortified herself with a slogan, "Aquafina. Purity guaranteed!" She paused and then yelped, "Aquafina. The sweet taste of purity!"

Rolling a blood red cranberry around in her mouth the Dutch woman spoke, "Zonder het vlees is alles verloren." [Without flesh all is lost.]

The woman thrust herself forward, almost leaning out of the frame. La Betty recoiled from the copper cup of wine offered to envelop the tongue, the warm velvet sleeve available at a touch, the fair plump cheek to pet, perhaps as prelude to slipping a hand further along to the loosened blouse and then beneath the blouse to slide along the smooth perfumed shoulder.

By gesture, by shifting her abundant skirts and by the look in her eye the young woman implied she would transport La Betty to a carnal lifestyle. With her every movement the young woman was signaling to La Betty, presenting a wordless promise, the promise of an endlessly sensual life.

La Betty shook her head again and again. In a little while, having recited "Ivory Soap. 99 and 44/100ths per cent pure" fifteen times La Betty was safely alone with the cold green gown.

French Forest

La Betty sat staring out the thirtieth-floor window of her condo overlooking English Bay. She savoured the effect of afternoon light streaming along her antique Fortuny dressing gown. Her eyes followed the hundreds of narrow pleats till the hem folded slightly against the carpet. As the clouds shimmered the glass and satin gown shifted to forest green, then pine green, then laurel green. And when the parting clouds revealed the sun, the classic "Delphos" daywear glowed chartreuse. The carpet too was influenced by the intense beams of light. This 19th century Sultanabad carpet was dominated by an enormous central rectangle of interwoven shades of muted green. The melange of foliage greens was enclosed by a narrow Imperial Yellow border teeming with stylized Persian purple jujubes and red Persian crown lilies. Scintillating as the frame was, especially in the sunshine, the hazy green rectangle dominated. Its melding greens suggested an endless meadow, or unnaturally tinted clouds, or strata of the sea.

The imposing ambiguous plane of green had always bothered La Betty. She just could not comprehend why a Persian carpet featured such an austere expanse, magnificently woven and palatially expensive, yet skimpy on decoration. La Betty had always believed that Middle Eastern carpets should be priced according to the number of decorative motifs per square centimeter. Yet when her great Aunt Ardie's father had acquired this Sultanabad the price had been 85,000 early 20th century American dollars.

La Betty glanced at the carpet's green vista. She was quite surprised to find a compelling impression of rippling green clouds. As with all clouds they rarely remain just clouds; forms emerge and dissolve. La Betty perceived an entire scene: a forest of a thousand different shades of green. New leaf green, hundreds of different mature leaves, mint green, pine green, sage green, and in the shadows midnight green. The trees, bushes, vines and undergrowth bordered an empty Imperial Yellow rectangle. As if the sun stood still, no shadows crossed the bright yellow patch. Its glow was constant.

An indistinct figure lingered in the shade. It was impossible to discern his clothes or to perceive his features. With an exasperated sigh, La Betty recognized the situation. She closed her eyes tight. She was blind to the forest and the human form, for a moment, but immediately the scene reappeared as a translucent vision behind her eyes.

A phantasm had arrived. Defiantly La Betty tried willing herself deaf, but the phantasm's moralizing was all too audible, "Tree planting is one of the most gratifying jobs—physically and mentally—that you will ever have. Discover what planting is really like: a gruesome yet extremely rewarding experience."

"Green perfumes," La Betty chanted,

"*Calyx* by Clinique (helps skin create its own internal water source!),
AquaAllegoria Herba Fresca by Guerlain (clean and chic!),
Dahlia Divin by Givenchy (Like an haute couture gown, it envelops with its divine enchantment!)"

The spectre, dressed in pickle-green rags, stepped onto the flat Imperial Yellow patch. He cast no shadow. His long skinny slippers left no footprints. La Betty had never learned anything about the mythical Green Man, and the head of this Green Man had been replaced by a Western Screech Owl. Myrtle green vines were curling out of the owl's eye sockets. The owl spoke with a tongue that fluttered like a Luna Moth, "God bless the tree planters and their confident cry, 'Aim for each day to be your biggest!' There's always the beauty of the landscape no matter the burning pain. Commit yourself to nurturing the forests that nourish the planet!"

"'Its style never changes. It stays on the offensive. That's the power of YSL *Red*,'" recited La Betty as she walked away from the Sultanabad.

She reached for the gold iPad lying on her antique Adirondack Old Hickory twig stand. She held up the iPad and took a selfie. She had tossed her hair, holding her head at an angle of disdain, stating, "The incomparable supermodel Wihelmina has cautioned, 'Impeccable style is a must. If you don't look the part, no one will want to give you time or money.'"

La Betty shoved open the 11th century Palace of Westminster oak doors to her Dressing Room. Lifting the Fortuny dressing gown above her ankles she rushed to her $48,486 USD Louis XV Gilt Mahogany Dressing Table. She picked up her Lignum Vitae cosmetic jar, sighing, "Sisleya L'Integral, $550 per 50 ml Persian acacia extract *promises*

> not to suffocate skin
> to comfort unhappy skin
> to reverse outbreaks
> to be magic fast!"

The Hit Man

La Betty's intercom connection to the doorman rang as delicately as Tinkerbell. Hearing it La Betty's heart began to tap dance in anticipation. La Betty was delighted a delivery was earlier than expected. All aflutter she didn't bother to instruct the doorman to tip the delivery guy fifty dollars and bring the packages to her door himself. She couldn't imagine how this Iranian Kashkoli Gabbeh rug she expected would be packaged. In moments she would be unwrapping a purchase, always a splendid amusement. La Betty waited to see whether the silk bonsai acacia tree she ordered had also arrived.

When the door of La Betty's condo was barely ajar her girlish openness turned into gray fear. A burly fellow had already gripped the door with one bulky forefinger. La Betty felt compelled to evaluate his flashy ring, the famous $8,000 Cartier 18k Gold Panther Band; then La Betty tugged sharply on the doorknob but couldn't pull the door shut. The stolid intruder had virtually cemented himself to the foyer's ebony wood floor. Strangely, the brute, who was not carrying any packages, did not try to enter. He was simply commanding La Betty's attention.

La Betty gave him the only attention she ever cared to offer. She evaluated the rest of the man's style. La Betty first noticed the fellow's Dolce & Gabbana black leather jacket. It was lambskin, supple with glints of blue light on the crests of folds. There were no scuffmarks on the rose gold studs and zipper.

The man, who was as stocky as a stump, looked too crude even to play rugby. Somewhat hunched and short of neck, he seemed most capable of unsportsmanlike violence. This aspect of his demeanor distracted La Betty from looking for the brand name of his pullover.

La Betty felt no impulse to speak. This boulder of manhood was so formidable that he was certainly insensitive to etiquette. La Betty feared even saying, "Good Afternoon" might enrage him.

"Look at the face," the brute said gruffly. La Betty's own facial expression became quizzical. La Betty looked.

The man's skull was almost cubical. His complexion was very peculiar, as if he'd eaten far too many carrots. The orange skin had just a slight sheen, like butcher paper.

La Betty, appalled by the very idea of skin, never mind a command to gaze upon it, began to shiver. She concentrated instead on the peridot eyes, eyes that didn't seem to see her. The proportion of iris to whites was abnormal. The irises were way too small. Something was amiss.

La Betty glanced surreptitiously at the top of the guy's head. The hair was sparse and looked uncommonly dull. She looked closer where the sides met the top. The brute was wearing a synthetic hair toupee.

"In Russia," said the bruiser, realizing La Betty was staring at the toupee, "In Russia we call it fish fur."

Haltingly in a monotone the questionable bruiser almost seemed to be reading, "If you want you can bring donger upon yourself. You can prov yourself. You got somping to prov? Fight to the death for pride. Rage. That's plenty enough."

La Betty was still staring at the toupee. She was quite worried that this monster, in one final attempt to intimidate her, would yank the toupee off his head. There could be burned skin or freshly slashed skin or a failed skin graft. Or maybe there wouldn't be any skin at all, just a hole full of blueberry Jell-O. Even if La Betty didn't see skin, she would imagine the worse skin ever.

This was the most mesmerizing visitation La Betty had ever endured. Her rebuke was stark, "A diamond is forever."

A tear shimmered in the fellow's sad eye. This tear was his last ploy and La Betty was not sympathetic. Now she was confident. La Betty knew: this was another perverse interruption. This thug was a phony. This guy, if he was, technically speaking, a human guy, was either a very inexperienced actor or, most likely, an apparition.

And so La Betty turned the tables on him. She took a deep breath, looked down at her royal blue fingernails, and began naming movie stars whose role was as psychopath in famously successful movies,

> Klaus Kinski, Al Pacino,
> Woody Harrelson, Dennis Hopper,
> Joe Pesci, Sharon Stone,
> Peter Lorre, Anthony Hopkins.

Already the phony hit man had turned his back. His head was bowed, toupee slipping forward. He was gliding away without moving his legs.

Silver Pink

La Betty walked into her "Kaffe Corner," a little rounded alcove at the east end of her condo. Its plastered walls were painted pale laurel green. La Betty wanted the walls repainted Silver Pink. Silver Pink was not shiny, not saccharine, definitely not Gucci "Valentine's Day Dionysus Super Mini-Bag" pink. Silver Pink was as if the early rays of dawn were reflected across a flawless silver plateau, emitting a momentary illusion of silver plus pink. The colour Silver Pink had been discovered by M. and Mdm. Plochere in 1948, but it could often actually appear in the early morning, across the sterling silver tray of La Betty's $9,612.15 Emile Viner coffee serving set. The tray would catch the light of dawn almost before the sky did. The convergence of rosy light and polished silver was as wondrous as the Transit of Venus, although La Betty herself had no idea there was such a thing as the Transit of Venus.

In readiness for this event La Betty would occasionally trouble herself to arrange the Koffe Corner just so. Today, Sunday the 21st, would be the morning for the enchantment; La Betty had already pushed one of her Osvaldo Borsani tables just a little closer to the window, positioned for dawn's first blush to hover across the flawless silver tray. La Betty was ready for the ritual, to conjure the evanescent marvel, silver plus pink.

In anticipation of sunrise La Betty moved across from the east window to her Ib Kofod-Larsen Danish 1950 teak sofa. Before sitting down, she skimmed her right hand across the blue velvet upholstery. La Betty's $5,156.05 Ceylon Blue Sapphire ring was like a moonlit shadow cast on the sofa's azure. It sent La Betty's eyelids aflutter. She sat on the sofa, smoothing her 1970s John Radaelli white laced linen skirt over her knees.

The sunbeams arrived. Within a moment the flicker of pink shifted into the silver gleam, then vanished. What a delicate, astonishing glimpse of the extraordinary colour! La Betty murmured, "I love it so. This is the perfect colour for an iconic fingernail polish."

The fugitive glow on the tray had left an ache of desire in La Betty's throat. She would look up and around at the walls of her Kaffe niche. She would imagine an Instagram image of her hands touching the wall. The wall would be an oceanic backdrop for her gorgeous silver pink nails.

"In other news today, the poet Stephen Crane has died. Plagued by financial difficulties and ill health, Crane died in a Black Forest tuberculosis sanatorium. Stephen Crane was 28." La Betty's literary education was rather shallow, and so she assumed Stephen Crane couldn't have been a celebrity poet like Maya Angelou. Regarding poetry itself La Betty did remember the easier rhymes, such as,

> Ride a cock-horse to Banbury Cross,
> To see a fine lady upon a white horse;
> Rings on her fingers and bells on her toes,
> And she shall have music wherever she goes.

The radio announcer began to read one of Stephen Crane's well-known poems. The announcer's voice was rather high-pitched and his rapid speech slurred, as if he was thrust into the job because the serious newscaster had actually just dropped dead in the broadcast booth.

The fellow read the poem in a monotone, as if there was no punctuation or indentation,

> I stood upon a high place and saw below many
> devils running leaping and carousing in sin one
> looked up grinning and said comrade brother

La Betty could not have been expected to enjoy a poem that didn't rhyme. Of more relevance she had totally missed that the announcer was a phantasm: Crane had died in 1900, twenty years before the very first radio news broadcast. But La Betty's apathy toward the history of technology was shielding her from the uncanny nuisance of this anachronism. As alert as she usually was to ghostly interventions, to the unwanted 20th century affirmations meant to reform her, this visitation was too subtle. Besides, La Betty's attention had been distracted immediately by the word "devils." She did not even notice the phantom radio had gone silent after the announcer finished saying the word "brother."

La Betty was already entertaining herself with her own silent recitation, listing the luscious Halloween lipstick colours she'd seen advertised alongside the website for Los Angeles Fashion Week October 2018,

> "Speak of the Devil
> Red Devil
> The Devil's Stare
> The Devil's Night Smoke
> Rose Gold Devil's Dust
> Dare Devil
> The Devil Wears Purple
> Lucky Devil
> Bloody Devil."

A Room with Blue Bedspreads

This is not La Betty's bedroom. This room is remarkable in ways that La Betty does not appreciate. In spite of Crayola blue and the depth of reminiscence that blue evokes, La Betty would be utterly unmoved by the simplicity of this place. La Betty would cringe at the bedspreads. Their blue is naked; the absence of ornamentation betrays frugality, a stance La Betty cannot bear.

Although La Betty wouldn't deign to enter this room, if she did she would cringe at the outdated television across from one of the beds. She would turn her back to it immediately. To La Betty a TV absolutely must be a 8K Ultra HD portal into the universe of fashion. Fashionable images are always shimmering and sumptuous. Fashion never sleeps.

La Betty would never step into this room. Seemingly different from her condo, this room no doubt harbours a potential threat, or, as La Betty would describe it, "a perverse interruption." Perverse interruptions have disturbed La Betty too often. La Betty won't go anywhere and risk a perverse interruption. So she won't go anywhere.

These so-called perverse interruptions emanate from very suspect sources. They are shape shifters. They are spectral enticements that perpetrate every possible inducement for La Betty to change her allegiance from consuming to participation.

La Betty has stabilized her lifestyle. Her condo is ten times the size of this blue-centered room. La Betty has quarantined herself voluntarily, to protect her pure devotion to shopping. The less La Betty's lifestyle changes the more secure she feels. La Betty has seen how often, beneath the surface of mundane rooms, festering in the shadows, are the insubordinate entities, phantoms of the twentieth century, resentful spirits that do whatever they can to lure La Betty away from love of Spectacle.

Undoubtedly such entities are in this Spartan room, probably hiding on—or in—the television screen. The trembling picture on the TV would probably be a "Buffy the Vampire Slayer" rerun. At an unforeseen moment, however, the program will be interrupted due to "technical difficulties." Then iconic TV "snow" will fill the screen. But this time the snow looks like a swarm of bees. The snow leaves the screen because it actually is a swarm of bees. The TV goes black and the swarm roars. The swarm spreads out like an overcast sky hovering just above the curtain rods. The layer of bees slowly descends. Finally the crowd is so thick it covers the blue beds with buzzing and shivering insects.

Then a single bee emerges from a swaying curtain. The bee enlarges. As it enlarges it is no longer a bee. It is an elongated moss-green four-footed reptile with the massive pink face of an unaccountably familiar infant. The baby opens its mouth and its nostrils close down like a crocodile's going under water. The baby's eyes bulge as it prepares to speak, although there is no person in the room to listen.

> Early in the movement it was the same. No one to listen. But as soon as one Pariah listened it was as if one spark ignited a pyre. The corpse of colonialism was burnt to ashes.

What a coincidence. This is exactly what La Betty does not want to ever happen to consumerism. La Betty hasn't thought it through but this is her unique and wordless dread: What if La Betty herself is beguiled into releasing a spark that burns materialism to ashes? What if La Betty unwittingly starts the conflagration that consumes consumerism? The only way to avert this calamity, or so La Betty thought, was to confine herself to her condo. She had assumed that when you always are thinking of shopping condo life would feel like ultra comfort, not captivity. La Betty was certain she could fortify herself with divine purchases. She would be perfectly unharmed surrounded by a force field of mass media. La Betty would never have predicted her eventual claustrophobia, nor could she have foretold endless spiritual combat.

La Betty's materialism transcends the needs and predicaments of humankind. To La Betty materialism is a calling. Only the elite graced with perfect nonchalance can practice true consumerism. La Betty quoted the new Shakespeare,

> All the world's a shop;
> And we are but customers in it.
> We have our entrances and exits;
> The best of us have many styles
> and money enough to obey our fancies.

La Betty fancied herself an icon of the consummate materialist. La Betty had been sanctified by the Truth: superficiality is ecstasy.

The Most Beautiful Dress in the World

La Betty had discovered the Schiaparelli 2016 Spring/Summer haute couture collection while browsing the Internet for a new teapot. La Betty had wanted an antique porcelain teapot. La Betty would not be researching the history of teapots, certainly not the history of porcelain. La Betty assumed it was enough to know her own criteria for a pleasing teapot: first of all it must be a few centuries old; secondly, it must be decorated with lots of gold, and third, as if not associated anyway with the first two criteria, have an exhilarating price. Once these criteria were fulfilled La Betty knew what she liked.

The Schiaparelli 2016 Spring/Summer high fashion collection had been extensively documented. That season each ethereal gown was decorated here and there with embroidered depictions of ordinary objects such as scissors, an asparagus bunch, a watering can, a 1963 Western Electric touchtone telephone.

And then a remarkable coincidence occurred. La Betty was admiring a long dilute lavender gown, and there, embroidered on the right breast of the bodice, was a flamboyantly ornate teapot. La Betty downloaded the catwalk photo and began enlarging it. Seeing this teapot in detail La Betty was intrigued how it looked so very French, a Monsieur de Clignancourt porcelain. It gave a serious impression. It was stodgy yet stately, with a heavy gold handle and a muscular gold spout.

More unmistakably French were the alternating mauve and gold vertical stripes ascending from a wide gold band around the base. The stripes alluded to military parades and riches beyond compare. Beneath the lid was a frieze with finely speckled gold background. Bloated white daisies, calla lilies full of spiders and blood red rosebuds dominated the foreground, along with obviously imaginary plants. The latter gold and mauve plants looked like a fusion of feather with viper tongue. There were also delicate sprigs that looked like desiccated gecko feet. Painted on the lid's gold knob was a single white blossom of sandbog death lily.

Within moments the calla lilies performed an illusion. They remodeled into bizarre teapots. These sheer white pots had a very delicate small diameter at the bottom. As a whole each one resembled the poisonous yellow oleander. The open mouth at the top of this unorthodox teapot accommodated hundreds of black spiders and their webs. There were two exquisitely serpentine handles.

La Betty immediately cringed at the idea of teapots. She would never have thought that they involved spiders, near-vipers, poisonous flowers or reptile toes. She didn't drink tea anyway. She had merely toyed with the idea of porcelain and elegance, even perhaps the idea of porcelain and extravagance, but, *en fin*, this needlework teapot reminded her that sometimes well-wrought things can be unnerving.

La Betty quickly returned her focus to the other Schiaparelli catwalk photos. In a moment she beheld the most beautiful dress in the world. The little white silk bodice was trimmed with close knit gold seashell shapes that encircled the waist, decorated the vertical seam between front and back, and conglomerated atop the narrow shoulder straps. On the front of the bodice the circumference of a very big circle was delineated by a dense strand of gold calico clamshells, gold keyhole limpets, gold periwinkles and more. Closed within the circle was an applique image of a stunning though unnaturally scarlet King's Crown Conch.

From the waist the gown descended floor-length in multilayered shallow blue silk tulle. The blue strata would float and sway with each footstep. Within the layers numerous delicately stitched sea creatures appeared and disappeared, tiny pink crabs, charming silver seahorses, little green ribbontails, dwarf purple sea stars and an assembly of sea weeds such as sea petal, sea whistle and rippleweed.

La Betty savoured the gown until the scene changed to an interview of the very model who had worn the gown that year. The interviewer was inquiring about the life of the model, whose only name was Litu. Litu had retired the day after she wore the King's Crown Conch dress. "Why?" the interviewer had asked. La Betty believed Litu's answer to be massively déclassé.

> "The King's Crown Conch dress was the most beautiful dress in the world," answered Litu. "All my life I had wanted to wear the most beautiful dress in the world. I had modeled hundreds of dresses. But that day, in that Schiaparelli gown, the obsession was finished. After wearing the most beautiful dress in the world I was free to be ordinary."

Queen Elizabeth II

La Betty was staring at a portrait of Queen Elizabeth II. The portrait was enormous, set in an elaborately carved frame. The frame was as imposing as a fortress. Its ornamental carvings featured voluptuous roses, curvaceous ferns, dainty butterflies and the waves of an ocean. All these forms were immobilized under a layer of gold leaf. Queen Elizabeth II's portrait conveyed to La Betty the pinnacle of happiness; the portrait displayed royalty as thoroughly superficial, a magnificent surface. La Betty considered naturalism, realism, super realism, hyperrealism and magical realism vulgar, especially for images of royalty, superstars and elite athletes. Not that La Betty was familiar with these art school terms. La Betty had intuitively defined what to her would be "the essence of eminence:" a flat image with background, middle ground and foreground collapsed onto one shallow plane.

The colour pink, the most trivial of colours, dominated this image of Queen Elizabeth II. Queen Elizabeth II's gown was tinted pink. There was barely a distinction between the intense pink backdrop and Queen Elizabeth II's intensely pink hair. The few faux shadows were pink. To complete the illusion Queen Elizabeth II's visage was an ovoid surface without contour. As if they were stickers her eyes, lips and gold earrings were set on the plane of Queen Elizabeth II's white face.

This magnificent regal figment was the highlight of La Betty's brain.

La Betty was happy in the knowledge that, as she said to herself,

> Queen Elizabeth II is a nobody. She is the perfection of Nobodyness. We see her tiara, her blue satin sash, her elaborate gold necklace, but her face is as it should be, expressionless, revealing nothing. There is nothing to be revealed. What luxury! What a stupendous fate! All we can say about her portrait is that it always looks like Queen Elizabeth II under gold crowns encrusted with the emeralds, rubies and diamonds of the realm. She must be Queen Elizabeth II because the animal fur she wears is hundred-year-old feral ermine. She is depicted with a diamond ring that is bigger and brighter than the morning star. The outside of Queen Elizabeth II is so glamorous and grand there's no room for an inside. To inhabit such an image is worth more than The Koh-I-Noor diamond which, if she commands, will be presented to her on a purple velvet pillow.

La Betty felt heavenly as she savoured how shallow Queen Elizabeth II could be whenever she wished—and especially when duty called.

La Betty got distracted by a tiny pearl button that rolled along the floor. La Betty instantly discerned it was not mere cultured pearl; its wild gloss was unmistakable. La Betty didn't recognize its origin; she had no idea what article of clothing it had fallen from. When La Betty leaned down to pick it up it wasn't a pearl button after all. It was a wee white noggin atop a slimy white tail. The noggin was pearlescent and bald. The shiny slimy tail began where there is usually a neck. This was not a natural species obviously. A bulb on a cord, it rolled along as cranium and tail without a torso. There were two thick-lidded globular blue eyes on the head, and a small round orifice that was probably a mouth.

"I need my big silver-handle magnifying glass," La Betty thought, "It's more powerful than the little pearl handle one." Then the white creature spoke words that were so astounding La Betty forgot the magnifying glasses. And she recognized exactly what was about to happen. She was beset again by yet another perverse interruption, another fiend inveigling her to forsake shopping. This was another ugly phantasm trying to rot La Betty's resolve. La Betty would have liked to squish it but the best she could do was hold her hands over her ears while the infidel squeaked,

> Queen Elizabeth II has skin. It is very white, revealing blue veins flowing like Lilliputian tributaries toward her heart. Queen Elizabeth II may cover almost all of the skin yet it is there under hosiery, gloves, high collars and long sleeves. Her face however is always exposed. Queen Elizabeth II does not care, but take a look, La Betty. Queen Elizabeth II's nose is like a mongoose all but lost in ninety-two-year old furrows. Her very own skin proves Queen Elizabeth II is not a nobody. Truthfully she is just another someone. She is after all a mammal and so are you.

Slice of Earth

La Betty was nearly drowned by a dream. She sank to the bottom of sleep, far far below the surface of wakefulness. La Betty was lying on the black sand, face down on a carpet of bubbles. La Betty was relieved that her mascara and lipstick were waterproof, but her antique green silk Fortuny dressing gown was sticky with salt water. Like king-size seaweed the gown rippled in the gentle currents. La Betty's baby harp seal fur slippers were ruined under a layer of wet grit. The Henri Matisse *Oceanie, La Mer* pattern on La Betty's Hermès scarf had been a reminiscence of Tahiti. Now the scarf was fluttering like a guppy, at last released to drift back to the Tuamotu Archipelago and revert to the mere sentiment it once had been. La Betty hadn't even seen it flow away. She was preoccupied by the dozens of red wagtail platies. The platies were mistaking La Betty's Tahitian Tan sunscreen for the edible aromatic algae the platies love. Opening her mouth and chanting beneath this nightmare La Betty desperately tried to ward off the platies with the only kind of hex she knows, ad copy,

> Glamorous Tahitian Tan,
> the black pearl, born in the waters of Tahiti
> at the Corner of Happy & Healthy.

La Betty had never learned to swim so she could only crawl along on her hands and knees. With her Fortuny dressing gown hiked up to her hips La Betty was moving slow as a clam.

After a long while and many onrushing schools of shrimp La Betty discovered a wall. The wall was divided horizontally into different layers of sediment, progressing upwards four layers from the darkest, kelp tea brown, to the thick speckled tan section. Sweet white seashells were scattered across the uppermost fine-grain layer of sand. As La Betty clawed and wriggled her way up layer by layer the waters beneath her evaporated.

La Betty was finally upright and dry. Strewn at the edge of an Adriatic Blue shallow pool La Betty spied bracelet charms: tiny white anchors, fishes, doves, a Chi-Rho, Jerusalem crosses, lambs and triangles. The carved details were exquisite. La Betty couldn't recall where she'd seen these symbols grouped together before, yet upon discovering them La Betty reflexively shuddered with a pang of suspicion.

This had not been, strictly speaking, La Betty's dream. La Betty was being dreamed by formidable persuasive entities. These phantasms too often beset La Betty. Always it is their mission to dupe La Betty into renouncing her lifestyle. Towing La Betty into this artificial, deceitful mimic of a dream these spiritual miscreants had expected La Betty to capitulate, to renounce superficiality and beg for spiritual depth.

Perplexed, now La Betty was standing in her condo bathroom. She was astounded to discover that her antique green silk Fortuny dressing gown was fresh and dry. Her feet were snug in feather-light baby harp seal fur slippers. Her mascara was not dribbling. Of course La Betty's moist lips were still creamy lavender, as anyone would expect from Guerlain Rouge G De Guerlain Jewel Lipstick. Realizing she had not gone anywhere at all La Betty's resentment escalated. It was entirely possible that evanescent Christian entities had enlisted The Holy Ghost to coerce La Betty's religious conversion. Those adorable charms on the sand were temptations placed by The Daemon of Light. The Daemon of Light was fierce and wily, but apparently It had not reckoned on La Betty's being genetically unfit to become poor in spirit, penniless or meek. The Daemon's mellifluous recitation from *The New Testament* was enunciated seductively, but the message itself was stale—and futile, "A man's life does not consist in the abundance of his possessions." This prosaic claim prompted La Betty to retort with the beefiest slogans she knew,

> Top power for the job.
> Better balance. Tougher, faster,
> more advanced. Angel grinder.

La Betty's thoughts harkened back to the charms. She wished she had gathered as many of them as she could. Of all the illusions that swirled through that dream, La Betty persuaded herself the delicate trinkets had been real. In hindsight La Betty regretted she'd left behind superbly rare ivory carvings. As epitomes of La Betty's incisive taste, they had to have been baubles with a breath-taking price. Gorgeous, rare, expensive: with these criteria confirmed, La Betty knew what she liked. If she had gathered up all those charms buying a new bracelet would have been crucial. La Betty imagined herself browsing the Tiffany & Company's website. La Betty was fond of rose gold, and a Tiffany's $2,500 oval link bracelet would be divine.

Ugly David

La Betty sat staring out the thirtieth-floor window of her condo overlooking English Bay. Day was drifting down to dusk. The water lay beneath the sky like a blue satin sheet. A vast pane of bone-white desert shimmered on the other side of the bay. Self-absorbed as La Betty usually is she certainly knew that the site of The Vancouver Maritime Museum is not a vast bone-white desert. The mirage was fascinating La Betty anyway, as if it was the set for an haute couture photoshoot. La Betty, however, had no idea how truly preposterous it was to see, in fact, this particular desert across the water. This vast pale plane was a mirage of Al-Wadi al-Jadid, the White Desert of Egypt. The Kharga, Farafra, Dakhla and Baris oases were identifiable as aquamarine squiggles.

La Betty peered at the Kharga Oasis squiggle and spied, as if looking through a telescope, a billboard between a stand of acacia trees and a cluster of thorn palms. La Betty's easily deluded mind could actually focus clearly on the billboard. La Betty perceived the billboard as extravagant film promotion: a scene from Werner Herzog's *Queen of the Desert* starring Nicole Kidman in a smoky lavender hijab, stumbling through a sandstorm with a herd of white camels.

A $1,300 Rag & Bone label "Duke" camel hair coat was hanging in La Betty's closet. Its history involves a secret kept in common with Nicole Kidman, who wore an identical one to the 2016 Metropolitan Museum of Art "Oasis Fashion Gala:" the "Duke" camel hair coat was designed for men but had been tailored into a bespoke women's coat. Remembering this La Betty felt shatter-proof.

La Betty rose from her authentic George Nelson "Coconut chair" and hurried to her closet. She was eager to hold the "Duke" in her arms. The coat felt so dreamy she decided to wear it. When La Betty returned to the window nighttime had transformed the window into a black mirror. La Betty anticipated her own image glorified by the magnificent "Duke." She was aghast to gaze instead upon a very uncool young man with an awful hairdo. Not a man, he was a paint-by-numbers print, set in a bargain basement LexMod armless chair. La Betty was offended by his Banana Republic khaki shirt and anonymous khaki trousers. His untrimmed 1990s "curtain" style haircut was ridiculous. La Betty was more than relieved this faux reflection had not usurped her face.

La Betty sighed in frustration. Mirrors don't lie, but bodiless hostile entities do. Once again, a phantasm had obviously entered her condo, determined as ever to convert La Betty to some selfless form of community participation. But no, La Betty completely identifies with *"Bling H2O luxury water*, in frosted bottles adorned with Swarovski crystals. Gold-filtered mineral water. Pure water. Pure gold. Pure bliss." La Betty put her hands in the "Duke's" pockets and stiffened her back. La Betty expected the intrusive imp, this useless visitation, would promote a career, something so very outré it hadn't been respectable since the early twentieth century.

The wraith began to speak, but the goofy young man-image dressed in khaki did not move his lips. He was a mere two-dimensional figure no thicker than his reflection. The weak whiny voice was not his. The voice was emanating from the 2017 fall issue of Luxury and Ornament magazine lying on a nearby 1930's

Parisian white leaded oak pedestal table. An article on page twenty-two listed "Ten Cool Haircuts for Men," beginning with "1. short textured crop, 2. short pomp, 3. comb over fade, 4. high fade, 5. burst fade Mohawk..." La Betty was definitely curious, but as soon as she heard the sappy words, "Librarians believe in change and..." La Betty interrupted aggressively with a Vera Wang declaration, "A great shoe or a great handbag or a great top or a great coat or jacket can change everything!"

La Betty glanced at the aquamarine squiggle tattoo behind the high fade model's ear. It became a withered pair of vertical lips, squeezing out the words of Gustave Flaubert, "Do not read to amuse yourself, or like the ambitious, for the purpose of instruction. No, read in order to live." The squeaky unwelcome phantom repeated, "Librarians believe ..."

"Maybelline!" snarled La Betty,

"Maybelline, Pantene,
Olay, Garnier,
Shiseido, Aveeno,
Clinique;

Coty, Vichy,
Revlon, Avon,
Nivea, Natura,
Dove;

Speed Sticks, Matrix
Kerastase, Kosé,
Oriflame, L'Occitane,
Christian Dior;

Bioré, Roche-Posay,
Schwarzkopf, Body Shop,
Clarins, Redken,
Clean&Clear!"

The Jester

La Betty's bedtime indulgences took an hour to complete. First her languid bath with a teaspoon of nourishing leaf-alga oil diluted by silky lime-infused mineral water. After her long bath La Betty wraps herself in a towel large enough to dry a titan. Its colours are soothing light and dark tans with flowing cream swirls, cozy and thick like a warm cappuccino. La Betty strokes her hair using a brush made with Argentinian *porco-do-mato* bristles. She stands quite a time savouring her gowns in the ylang-ylang scented closet. On this night she chooses an antique green silk Fortuny dressing gown.

La Betty had been asleep in her bed for five hours when the clinking of little bells woke her. La Betty was discombobulated. She could not decide whether she was actually still asleep. If she was asleep the dream bells would continue to ring. If she was indeed awake and opened her eyes supposedly there would be silence.

La Betty's pillow seemed somehow to become a big marshmallow. The icing sugar powdered her face. Shaking her head La Betty opened her eyes. She could see lavender marshmallows attached to a broad leather strap that was itself attached to an unusual single-string instrument. La Betty was very surprised she hadn't immediately noticed there was also a muscle-bound giant flaunting the peculiar instrument. The giant was dressed like a Renaissance merry-maker. Or perhaps his costume was a mockery of the Vatican Swiss Guard. The giant's red and black satin pants were in fact very short puffy bloomers. Thirty gold buttons were attached to the sumptuous matching jacket.

"Marshmallows are so jolly! Jollier than jolly," exclaimed the giant. He shook the leather strap. Some marshmallows drifted away and others held on, ringing like bells.

The huge jester plucked the instrument's single string. The sound it made was of a breeze over a dainty pond. For an instant a sweet-smelling fog filled La Betty's bedroom. When the giant quaked with laughter the fog disappeared. The giant chirped, "sweet-smelling frog!" The giant reached over to fetch a sweet-smelling frog from behind some purple drapery. He then lost himself in a joyous roar. He plucked the string again—the marshmallows drifted away.

Next the mischievous giant unbuttoned his jacket. Under the jacket La Betty was not sure what she saw, whether a rough dark wool undergarment or the giant's dense dark chest hair. La Betty looked away quickly. Doing so, by turning her head, she was facing a stuffed pallid pink flamingo standing on one scrawny leg. "Ding-a-ling a-ling," the flamingo peeped.

The jovial giant smiled. The cheer in his smile was as if there was peace on earth. He announced he would sing a love song. La Betty cringed, thinking "Not for me no sirree. No! Please not for me." The giant nodded warmly as if he had heard her thoughts.

"I am at my best singing a love song," he said, "Baritone love ditties are irresistible, and so they should be. The lyrics are somewhat rhythmic and also somewhat rhyme." This incited the flamingo to laugh so heartily it had to flap its bony wings to stay upright. The giant too was giggling hysterically yet he began to sing,

> Oh, pretty one, let us joke
> Joke the ripper undid his zipper
> He brought giddiness just for you
> And gaudiness too
> You, my sweet, could use a laugh
> And a bath, you do the math
> We'd like you to smile
> We'd walk a mile
> to see your white teeth
> and the pink gums beneath...

La Betty recognized this calculated temptation, this offer of eternal silliness, this seduction away from all the pretty things that keep her pure. She knew what the muscle-bound jester wanted from her—to abandon her shopping, and for what? His eyes twinkled all right, but it was a signal that he was only pretending.

La Betty pulled one of the pillow-size marshmallows over her eyes. Muffled but adamant she chanted the protective names of haute couture fashion houses:

> Kenzo, Fendi,
> Calvin Klein, Givenchy,
> Comme des Garçons, Coach 1941,
> Valentino, Dior,
> And Yves St. Laurent.

The giant was gone and La Betty's pillow marshmallow was now becoming a very plump Barbie-pink flamingo. Its legs were tucked under and La Betty's head nestled into its warm abundant feathers. The pink down powdered her face. Her determination and faith were a solace; the giant had been testing what he could get away with. La Betty was no fool.

Temptation in the Desert

La Betty sat staring out the thirtieth-floor window of her condo overlooking EnglishBay. The September rain had been falling for three days. Late at night, seen from above, the raindrops on the water looked like the boiling bubbles in a cauldron of purple-black *Feijoada Brasileira*. La Betty picked up her gold iPad to linger momentarily over a colour photo of this darkly robust soup. Unexpectedly, the screen switched to a black and white image. It was Luiza Maranhão in a scene from the 1961 Brazilian film *A Grande Feira*. La Betty had always tried to guess what colour Miss Maranhão's fitted waist décolleté tight skirt might have been, considering Dior had favoured pink that year. In this scene from *A Grande Feira* Miss Maranhão is walking down a spiral staircase with an ivory-handle straight razor in her hand. Her beautiful black face suggests revenge.

La Betty rose from her George Nelson black leather and steel "Coconut" chair. She stood at the window looking past the raindrops slipping down the glass. Beyond the glass and rain La Betty could discern the full moon. It was perfectly round, sweet and soft like a Brazilian *sequilhos de maizena*. La Betty likened the *sequilho* to Dior's New Look Cartwheel hat. For years La Betty had admired the 1940 Alfred Eisenstadt photo of Stephanie Nikashian on Copacabana Beach. In the photo Miss Nikashian is clad in a straw cartwheel hat, wearing sunglasses with seashell rims as she suns in her Turkish trousers and blouse. La Betty would always be happy knowing Stephanie Nikashian's image in those seashell-rimmed sunglasses is immortal, on the internet.

La Betty's gaze returned to English Bay. She couldn't believe her eyes. The water looked like the languid sands of Copacabana Beach. As if they were thousands of voodoo pins the raindrops were piercing and stinging the sand.

A seven-eighths naked, marvellously proportioned man emerged from the surf and walked to a deserted beach umbrella. He sat under it, and somehow he was cradling the famous Caîpirinha *cachaça* cocktail in his large, strong right hand. The drink was garnished with a slice of lime just as when Miss Nikashian had drunk it through a straw in a coconut shell. The man wore a large rigid loin cloth like Lex Barker's in the 1949 movie *Tarzan and the Magic Fountain*. He was, however, not a man. La Betty's solitude was once again being distorted by an obnoxious phantasm. She watched the apparition remove his loincloth; it was instantly replaced by an unintelligible pixilated rectangle. La Betty loathed this disjointed oceanside vista; it felt as if it was orchestrated by a Cubist demon. The apparition looked into La Betty's eyes as if she was under the umbrella with him. He spoke Portuguese.

> "Venha comigo para o Hotel Fountainebleau. Você será inspirado irresistivelmente pelo Chef!"*

La Betty countered,

> "The Blonde Salad™ introduces Fruity™ beauty lipstick with delicious fragrances! Fruity™ beauty! Fruity™ beauty!"

---

* "Come with me to the Hotel Fountainebleau. You will be irresistibly inspired by the Chef!"

As if in rebuttal the wraith shouted the authentic ingredients of JFK salad dressing:

> "5 whole eggs!
> 1 clove garlic!
> 1 teas salt!
> ¼ teas pepper!
> 2 tbsp paprika!
> 1 teas prepared mustard!
> 3 cups salad oil!
> 1 cup olive oil!
> ½ cup red wine vinegar!"

The holographic muscle man obviously admired the Fountainebleau chef who had invented the JFK salad dressing. In 1960 The President had dined at the Fountainebleau. La Betty either didn't notice or didn't care that the spectre was talking about Miami, not Copacabana Beach.

The spectre set the empty coconut shell on the sand. He reached for a nearby turquoise Bakelite transistor radio. The radio was broadcasting Chef Mario Batali baring his deepest motivations, "Although the skills aren't hard to learn, finding the happiness and finding the satisfaction and finding fulfillment in continuously serving somebody else something good to eat, is what makes a really good restaurant."

"Imagine the power," said the phantom, "the power of Jian Heng Loo, the current Chef at the Fountainebleau. He can import live white King Ivory Gulls from Norway. They are kept alive, are in quite high demand, sold at $600 a serving."

"A bold Givenchy lipstick makes me feel invincible," La Betty declared as one by one she studied the Butter™ Fruit Machine cherry-red-gumball lacquered fingernails of her right hand.

Forefinger:	NOT Lex Barker.
Second finger:	clingy ill-fitting transparent food-handler gloves
Middle finger:	the origin of the gloves involved:
Ring finger:	reworking the formula for condoms.
Little finger:	cutting into dead birds.
Thumb:	"finding fulfillment?" Fulfillment is for the little people.

Black Treasure

La Betty strode into a spacious unfurnished room. Her pulse accelerated as she anticipated how the room might soon be decorated. The alabaster walls were as yet unpainted. Ornate carpets soon would illuminate the pale enameled floor. Twenty feet overhead the ceiling had been finished with gray tumbled-slate tiles, a whimsical project, as the gorgeous tiles had been produced for use as flooring. There were only two pieces of furniture in the room, an $11,842 Adolf Loos 1931 walnut wood armchair and an elegant French Empire *bureau-plat* desk with an *or moulu* laurel wreath on each of four drawers. Below each corner of this mahogany desk a prominent blue porcelain caryatid was set at the top of each leg. A blue porcelain anklet encircled each leg ending with a highly stylized silver feline foot. In 1830 the dark lustrous desk had been crafted daintily, while its hefty blue and gold ornaments were explicitly pompous.

La Betty did not sit in the handsome chair. Its cocoa brown velvet cushion was so deep and stiff it filled the entire cubical space between the arms and the bottom frame. This disproportion was wry somehow, yet convivial, like a puppy whose head is too big.

La Betty walked directly to the desk. She pulled open the front drawer, reached in, and extracted a large blue and gold vintage Hermès silk scarf labeled *Tresors de*

Benin. Golden images of mysterious statues were arrayed symmetrically around a central depiction of a strange gleaming hut. The statues were sheltered by large Royal Blue feathers, grasses and leaves. The only other colour was the raw umber skin of a young man sitting among reeds, and on the opposite corner of the carré a deity in her ceremonial horn-shaped headdress. La Betty assumed these half-naked figures were large ebony statues adorned with gold jewelry. Figures of a cockerel and of a fang-baring panther were also illustrated in gold.

La Betty savoured the thought of owning a gold panther statuette. She naturally assumed that *Tresor de Benin* was a Parisian antique emporium; it would no doubt have a website. She pictured the miniature panther placed in this unfinished room, echoing the gold and blue features of her French Empire desk. Obviously La Betty's enthusiasm for outstanding objects took precedence over their history, or any history of anything whatsoever, for La Betty's world was an array of objects as vast and, in a sense, as timeless, as the Milky Way. She studied a price tag as a historian investigates a date, and for La Betty the date, such as "1931 Adolf Loos armchair," was an arcane reiteration of the price.

La Betty raised the scarf, holding it before her eyes as if it was a famous oil painting. As it fluttered slightly the panther shivered and its mouth seemed to reveal more of its golden fangs. The subtle undulation of the panther's head conveyed a frown, a disturbing unsympathetic frown. Now the Royal Blue fronds seemed to part, rustling audibly as they freed the panther from their shadows. Yet the panther, released from the shadows, darkened to the colour of Royal Blue, then darker still, midnight blue, darker still, black shimmering blue. As the panther's body darkened the rustling loudened to hissing, and then to sizzling and crackling.

Now La Betty frowned, a disturbing unsympathetic frown. She resented her splendid Hermès scarf being possessed by a bodiless entity, a perverse interruption.

Next she could expect some wraith whispering pointless 20th century affirmations, earnest advice soaked in silly humanist nostalgia.

Suddenly the silky scarf swept into her face. It was as if its gold was burning like the sun; La Betty's reflex was to grasp the corner of scarf angrily, to rumple it inside her bony white fist. She willed herself deaf, but this time the twentieth century declaration was visual: although the gold words on the blue silk border of the scarf still read *Tresor de Benin*, every deep blue leaf shone with another message, *If you have uniforms we will have uniforms. If you have attack dogs we will have attack dogs. If you have rifles the Black Panther movement will have rifles. This is equality.*

La Betty dropped the scarf to the floor. She began to chant,

> "Flap Bag Chanel.
> Chanel Flap Bag Chanel:
> *This black beauty*
> *This black beauty*
> *is the perfect size.*
> *This black beauty*
> *is the perfect size.*
> *Every woman needs a Chanel*
> *in her handbag arsenal.*

Ghost

La Betty sat staring out the thirtieth-floor window of her condo overlooking English Bay. A sailboat gala was enlivening the waters. At least thirteen spotlights were criss-crossing the darkness. The streams of light would expose sails for a moment of perfect glare. Festoons of little red, blue and green lights twinkled across the decks. The boats were swaying in place as their passengers waved greetings with their white handkerchiefs. Sparkles intermingled with swaths of darkness like handfuls of diamonds on deep blue velvet. For La Betty this jubilant event evoked images of fashion shows in the '30s, when dresses were as delicate as damselfly wings. La Betty looked across the room at an original 1938 Horst P. Horst photograph. It portrayed a slinky woman modelling a Madam Vionnet gold lamé sheath dress with a transparent net overskirt. Shifting back and forth between dazzle and dark the sailboats looked as lissom as the Vionnet gown.

La Betty leaned back to relax in her black leather George Nelson "Coconut" chair. She suddenly remembered that she had set the autumn 2018 issue of Ornament & Luxury magazine on the white leaded oak pedestal table to the right of her chair. She began leafing through it, eager to discover the latest elegantly expensive clothes and accessories. Strangely, the glossy pages reflected the sparkling streaming lights of the water below. This lent an incongruous aura to page 113, the amusing regular feature "Good Riddance," presenting a previous trend that had fallen into the abyss of bad taste. The article displayed the cover of the 1955 October #13 issue of Casper the Friendly Ghost. Casper the character was not considered outré; the outfit Casper was wearing was seriously third-rate.

Somehow in spite of Casper's incorporeal state the tacky outfit he wore did not fall off or through him. Casper was topless, wearing red Bermuda shorts with huge white polka-dots. The green clasp-style buckle secured a narrow blue belt. Casper's beanie had wide red and orange stripes. The commentary filled half the page. Maybe it was sardonic, but La Betty didn't care. She quickly focussed on the feature "Immortal," on the opposite page. There she saw the dramatically divine "Ghost Wedding Dress" from Viqing Vin's Paris 2012 spring/summer collection. It was as if the model was wearing the Milky Way. La Betty never remembered anything at all from common parlance or she would have mused "From the ridiculous to the sublime," but even casual commentary was to her a waste of time. She was happiest when she could madly adore an haute couture creation.

Then La Betty felt something pinching her right ear like a crude 1950s clip-on earring. La Betty, whose ears were pierced, reached for the earring gingerly. It was one of those dangling $465 Gucci silver ghost earrings. It was wriggling but La Betty was able to loosen it from the wee hole in her ear. When she held it in her hand, it was warm and moist like a frog in the sun, and it didn't stop squirming. La Betty felt not one instant of doubt: this was yet another perverse interruption. For certain there was a brazen phantom jiggling this bauble. The Gucci icon ghost trinket leaped from La Betty's hand and, slinging its silver chain, hopped onto the image of the Viqing Vin wedding dress. The trinket then melted into a tiny pearlescent wren's egg. It rolled off the magazine onto the pedestal table and trilled like a bird, whistling the words of Sophocles, "Children are the anchors that hold a mother to life."

The wishful thinking conveyed by this sentence, in spite of the egg's plaintive Edith Piaf warble, was just as repulsive to La Betty as holding a warm, moist frog.

The phantasm continued its Edith Piaf vibrato, "As the prophet Kahil Gibran reminds us, 'The most beautiful word on the lips of mankind is the word *Mother*, and the most beautiful call is the call of our Mother.'"

La Betty walked over to sit on the white Icelandic Eiderdown duvet enveloping her bed. She pulled her "Cappuccino Foam"-tinted calfskin footstool closer. Scornfully she kicked off her pink lambskin moccasins. She reached for her baby harp seal fur slippers. She slid a hand in each slipper and pressed them to her cheeks, buffing in circles ever so gently. She pouted awhile, then snarled,

> Fresh glow *Serenity Ocean*™
> Ultimate diamond dew infusion
> Hydrosparkling glimmering moisture
> A gem's glint; be the pearl in the oyster
> Twirl, glide, shine!

The Barber of Meadowlake

The Dior collection runway event would appear on YouTube, but the images would not be flat enough for La Betty; La Betty preferred colossally retouched still shots of humans, even black and white pictures, on condition they did not accentuate skin texture. La Betty recoiled at three-dimensional verisimilitude, and thus she was cautious deciding which shows to watch on her laptop, her 8K Ultra HD TV, her iPhone or her iPad. La Betty felt disdain toward fashion show videos. The hustle bustle, the jumble of colours, the loud apparently hip music filtered through worshipful commentary, this excitement was to La Betty an undulating nest of stinging insects. La Betty could not and would not concede that even in the digital era video should be considered necessary for contemporary websites.

La Betty adored viewing images of people stationary as silent icons. Naturally La Betty could be wild about select three-dimensional material objects, especially if the stylishness of their documentation aroused La Betty's will to possess. But it was as impossible as it was offensive for La Betty to identify with moving, talking humans.

La Betty was a loyal fan of *Vogue*.com's documentation of seasonal haute couture collections. La Betty was grateful that *Vogue*'s gorgeous colour photographs of motionless models had continued to be popular. The torpid statuesque models in artificially elegant poses were the apex of sophistication—safely and immeasurably superficial.

This year's photographs of the Christian Dior Fall collection enthralled La Betty. Each beguiling photograph ushered La Betty into a state of bliss. La Betty would savour the colours, the structure and the mien of each costume. The fixed painted faces of the models never quite reminded La Betty of humans. Each outfit could be experienced as an inorganic object.

La Betty was studying a dreamy dress. The ankle length skirt was subtly bell-shaped, with a wide waistband and a dark thunderously purple skirt. The colour of the tight long sleeve top was Japanese Black Plum. The blond model's face was anemic. Her eyes were pitiless blue ice. The model's hair was as white as Andy Warhol's wig, cropped somewhat roughly and short, almost as tousled as a stork's nest. At the bottom of the photograph, oddly, in tiny font, La Betty read, "Coiffure by the Barber of Meadowlake, barberofmedowlake.com."

Ordinarily a hairstylist would not be credited in Dior runway photos. Curious, La Betty typed in the website address. The website was, it seemed at first, a photo of a barbershop mirror. The mirror was decorated with a tortuously carved dark walnut frame. The reflection in the mirror was of the window to its right, and also the reflection of a reflection of the hair tonic bottles on the shelf in front of the mirror. Startled, La Betty glimpsed a reflection of a man, or a pale marble bust of a man. His shirt seemed lightly starched. Remarkably a lit cigarette drooped from the sculpture man's lips. And more remarkably every strand of the sculpture man's white hair was precisely the same as the Dior model's.

La Betty instantly concluded that the sculpture man was a ghost, a forlorn, disillusioned weakling, a spiteful imp determined to bewitch La Betty. These perverse interruptions by aggressive anti-consumerist phantoms too often appeared when La Betty was most serenely happy; when La Betty was most settled in a materialistic trance. Now La Betty was alerted and scornful. She braced herself to foil this presumptuous spirit by uttering a litany of powerful slogans,

> Enjoy the power.
> Pure water. Pure gold. Pure bliss.
> It takes the waiting out of wanting
> whatever makes you happy,
> Purely You.

The listless sculpture man inhaled deeply. The end of the cigarette glowed like a stoplight. The sculpture man raised the cigarette above his head while exhaling a grand silver cloud. "Face it," he spoke melodiously, "There's really nothing worth wishing or working for. You will live longer when you're apathetic. You can smoke and drink shamelessly; forget the whole damn thing." La Betty's rebuttal was forceful,

> Take time out for beauty.
> Not only looks better, but just is.

La Betty was chagrined that she could not remember the name of the car company that had presented this slogan to tempt customers.

The sculpture man lurched as if the word *beauty* was a jolt of electricity. He dissolved upwards into the dozens of grand silver clouds. La Betty slammed down the lid of her laptop like a woman slamming shut a window, a window that belongs exclusively to her.

Stone and Coil

There is a solid square jewelry box on an Osvaldo Borsani table in La Betty's bedroom. The lower half of the box is wrapped in stone gray satin. The satin-wrapped lid is burnt umber.

If we imagine the bottom of the jewelry box as a cube of rough marble and the top of the box as a carefully wound coil of thick dark wire, we can review what a phantom psychoanalyst explained to La Betty. The psychoanalyst was intent upon tempting La Betty away from her obsession with advertising. He wanted her to concede to the theory of neurosis accounting for her obsession. He was enticing La Betty toward an acknowledgement of her embryonic Super-Ego, and he expected her to discover she was only pretending to ignore her Id.

First the psychoanalyst had stated, "Behind every neurosis is the fear of Death." The psychoanalyst informed La Betty that the human mind dreads experiencing something utterly unprecedented. To this he had added that the human psyche is terrified by something against which it is entirely helpless. The mixture of these two absolutes instills a horror of the idea of Death when realistically no experience of actually being dead is possible.

La Betty hadn't comprehended any of these psychoanalytic pronouncements and that is why it took her some time to recognize that the psychoanalyst was a miserable tempter, a phantom killjoy whose motives were hostile.

"Consider this rough-cut cube of marble," the tempter continued, "It must be a symbol of death. See how it reminds one of something obdurate, something that neither negotiates nor cooperates. Intrinsic to the stone you will find no natural motive force, no transformative impulse. We must concede this marble cube is solid, heavy, and in a word inorganic. Allegorically this stone is as dispassionate as Death."

The psychoanalyst proceeded to describe how Freud discovered the Death Instinct. Freud had been bewildered by his analysands who would not equate health with an increase in the Pleasure Principle. His analysands would behave in ways that made them weaker and more ineffective. What was this?

Late one night Freud found himself contemplating the fragment of a stone Egyptian obelisk from his collection of antiquities. Suddenly he grasped what exactly he had been pondering: there must be an inclination, a tendency, a drive in all living things to undo the Eros of living, a drive to undo what the Will had attained.

Without any knowledge of DNA, Freud conjectured that every living creature is born with an impetus to undo itself. As Freud examined the obelisk fragment he suddenly understood: yes, the obelisk was carved and inscribed with human significance, but it was in essence a lifeless, unknowing chunk of stone. Thus the Death Instinct was revealed! Like artful engraving on lifeless marble all living beings are elemental atoms and concatenated molecules. Inherently, underneath the allure of artful engraving a clump of molecules is the substrate for an uncivilized desire. The Death Drive oxidizes the organic component until we are once again a mesh of passive molecules, until we are once again stripped to the substrate. In our ordinary lives day after day the Death Drive is edging us toward the ultimate apathy: an inorganic state.

The phrase "inorganic state" alerted La Betty that she was being courted intellectually by an insidious entity. In the guise of psychoanalyst this entity, as does every invading entity, was trying to shake La Betty's faith in the power of shopping. Although basically she had no comprehension of this Freudian logic, La Betty was repulsed by the idea of slumping into an inorganic state. This seemed like something not worth knowing, especially when La Betty had gathered for herself the ways, objects and supports to live undistracted by theories, hypotheses and ugly ideas.

Surprisingly La Betty did not assert a famous advertising slogan. With her lipstick she drew a square on the Osvaldo Borsani table and drew a ribbon wrapped around it, and a bow. She told the psychoanalyst "A square box can be a package from Bergdorf's in New York City."

The entity sloughed off his psychoanalytic mien. Now he looked like a hairless opossum, from whose drippy mouth the last of the psychoanalytic exposition melted into babble,

"If we take a mumble to consider the sprout of wire on top of this garbled cube, we see that it too disguises the cone of death. All oblivious features are ought within the moral coil. And upon what does the coil gape? Depth."

Down in the Mines

Evening veiled the sky over English Bay. In her condo on the thirtieth floor, watching the sunsets, La Betty would usually play a memory game: which emerging or dissolving colour had been worn by which supermodel or famous actress? This evening the sun and La Betty were as wan as Bartlett pears, sallow beneath a peculiar scrim of ash gray clouds. La Betty looked down at her Kashkoli Gabbeh carpet. Unlike the sky that night, the number of Kashkoli Gabbeh colours looked infinite. La Betty focused on the darkest colour, the expanse of phthalo blue. Across this blue, crimson squares, scarlet tulips, cerise stars and ruby X's seemed suspended over an abyss.

The thought of an abyss unnerved La Betty. She impulsively walked toward a closet door and pulled it open. The deep walk-in closet was lightless, which it was not supposed to be. The motion detector had failed. Blinded for a moment by the blackness La Betty didn't move. But within seconds this blunt darkness reminded La Betty of the Ralph Lauren Grecian-cut black velvet dress Kate Moss had worn for the 1996 cover of *Bazaar*. The Ralph Lauren noir had been uncompromising, as was the opaque blackness of La Betty's closet.

As La Betty stood there waiting for her eyes to adapt to the dark, she gradually perceived a glimmer at the far end of the closet. She walked cautiously toward it. The closet seemed to extend lengthwise until, seemingly a city block later, the glimmer proved to be quite an impressive circle of metallic light. The light flooded the rough wall of a deep cave. The stream of light was gushing from a huge lamp affixed to a miner's hardhat. The miner was standing motionless, as if he had accomplished something significant just moments before. Another miner was sitting on a nearby rock. At their feet La Betty discerned the word *dynamite* on a box. The circle of light had compacted these figures into silhouettes. La Betty interpreted the scene as a melodramatic ad for safety boots or perhaps rubber aprons.

La Betty's suspicion surged soon enough. It became obvious to La Betty that invasive entities were creating this dramatic mirage. La Betty surmised from experience that these faceless figures were definitely phantoms with an insulting agenda. Their rugged standardized outfits were evidence of their intent to undermine La Betty's devotion to the spectacular. La Betty dreaded being taunted or perhaps reproached. La Betty asserted a pre-emptive defense, quoting Edith Head, "You can have anything you want in life if you dress for it." La Betty was proud, her way of life was proof of this.

The miners aligned side by side and began to walk toward La Betty. She couldn't understand how she was once again at the door of her closet watching the two of them march closer and closer. At arms' length many details became more obvious, especially the canaries. What La Betty had perceived as lamps had been plump gold canaries. They sang,

> Union man! Union man!
> He must have full dinner can!
> AFL, CIO calling strike, out we go!
> We all contract, but it expire:
> union men is mad like fire;
> Miner strike takes too much time,
> Uncle Sam take over mines.
> After striking twenty days

we signing contract, we get raise.
Grocer comes and ringing bell
he raises prices—what the hell!
Union man! Union man!
He must have full dinner can!
AFL, CIO calling strike, out we go!" *

Shoulder to shoulder the miners shouted with black dust on their breath. They coughed "Solidarity!" in La Betty's face. And then they began to chant, "Loyalty. Loyalty. Loyalty. Loyalty. Loyalty to comrades a way of life!" La Betty slammed the closet door shut. She fortified herself repeating what Diana Vreeland had professed, "You must have style. It helps you get up in the morning. It's a way of life"

La Betty would never understand the advice or warnings imposed upon her by these perverse interruptions. To her their harangues conveyed prejudice or envy, or both. These self-righteous undead pests must be spirits from the twentieth century. These deathless losers were dragging around affirmations entire populations had failed to live by. Remembering Coco Chanel's discovery, "The sky is fashion," La Betty gazed beyond the window into the Ralph Lauren *noir* night.

---

* "Union Man," by George Korson, sung by Albert Morgan. Recorded in the Newkirk Tunnel Mine, Tamaqua, Pennsylvania, 1946

Head

La Betty sat staring out the thirtieth-floor window of her condo overlooking English Bay. A piercing red sunrise had dissolved into pallid early morning. Lounging calmly in her green antique Fortuny dressing gown La Betty sipped Tieguanyin tea. Her 18th Century German Porcelain cup and saucer glimmered sweetly on a 1930's Parisian white leaded oak pedestal table. The teacup's hand-painted bulbous little rose was looking surprisingly wan in the morning light. La Betty was puzzled that a rosy blossom could ever so subtly become overcast. She watched the flower beginning to quiver and then to darken. Its darkened shape became gray as wet cement. And it was no longer floral. The tiny form was converting to a somewhat triangular mass, as if it was a miniature painting of a monument on a cheap souvenir cup. The sculpted memorial stone had been carved into a disquieting face, inviting comparison with the big white men's heads of Mount Rushmore. This monument's features were astounding: the majestic nose, the substantial cheekbones, the look of panic in the widened eyes.

La Betty quickly looked away from the eyes and the gasping mouth, quickly looked away into the distance, as far into the Pacific Ocean as she could perceive. She was unnerved and restless, and she was guessing an unsympathetic wraith was entering the room, not, unfortunately, a rare occurrence. Yes, the visitations continued. This imp was floating somewhere, drifting behind La Betty as she tried to calm herself. She whispered cosmetic slogans as protective affirmations, "Short, dark and intense. Short, dark and intense. Quantum mascara brush. Short, dark and intense."

Her right hand had remained motionless holding the teacup while her left hand was groping around the top of another white leaded oak table on the left side. The touch of La Betty's forefinger identified the summer issue of *Ornament and Luxury* magazine. She turned her face and right hand away from the tea cup and gripped the magazine, leafing through it quickly to find the chandelier ad copy she had anticipated reading when she'd finished her tea. She laid the open magazine across her lap.

La Betty didn't recognize any of the pages. It was as if she was looking at an entirely different magazine, and this was enough to amplify La Betty's tension. She couldn't yet see the intrusive wraith. She knew it was nearby, but she was only able to sense its hissing. La Betty was increasingly bothered. She dreaded that the imp's hissing would, in all probability, coalesce into an annoying sermon or manifesto, or a creed, perhaps a homily.

"As Albert Einstein said, 'It is the supreme art of the teacher to awaken joy in creative expression and knowledge.'" The phantom spoke these words as it poured itself into the gleaming shape of a porcelain bear. This faux ornament perched on the "Cappuccino Foam"-dyed calfskin footstool that La Betty had used to fit into her baby harp seal fur slippers. La Betty didn't notice the beautiful bear. She certainly did not notice that it was back-to-back with a naked cherub holding a tambourine. Maybe La Betty would recognize this porcelain creation as the authentic 1914 $1,250 Rosenthal Bear & Child Porcelain Figurine by Ferdinand Liebermann; she might instinctively reach out to grab it—and be completely embarrassed to find it a deception, her greed completely frustrated. La Betty, however, was concentrating intently, trying to remember who Albert Einstein was. She knew, or thought she knew, that he was dead.

"Teaching is a very noble profession that shapes the character, caliber and future of an individual. Children must be taught how to think, not what to think. Teach the ignorant as much as you can; society is culpable in not providing a free education for all, and it must answer for the darkness which it summons." The phantom was quoting famous champions of education.

The implication was obvious: La Betty could respond sympathetically to the inspiration of venerable sages. La Betty could become a teacher. She could devote herself to curious young minds, infuse her students with the joy of learning—and La Betty could change their lives—and the way she lives.

La Betty could have screamed, "No! Never!" Instead she repelled the meddlesome wraith by chanting the sacred words of Christian Dior,

> "The tones of gray, pale turquoise and pink will prevail. The tones of gray, pale turquoise and pink will prevail. The tones of gray, pale turquoise and pink will prevail. The tones of gray, pale turquoise and pink will prevail."

Athlete with Barbell

There was someone at her window. La Betty stared at the pane just as she stares at any screen. She then glanced quickly at the screen in her hand, gauging the relative allure of the figure in the window compared to a Fendi pink python purse on www.BagTrend.com. The tiny figure at the window was standing so very still. He was a miniature strongman, holding his barbells with familiarity and respect. The strongman was floating 105 meters above the street, perfectly visible outside the clean condo window on the thirtieth floor. He was more than half naked in red boxer shorts. Neither cell phone nor wallet bulged in his pockets. His boxer shorts had no pockets. He was barefoot. His skin was as smooth as a peeled mango. Then, as if the strongman was being Photoshopped, the colours of his body, boxer shorts and bar bells began intensifying till they glistened like jellybeans.

The strongman was ogling the big crimson patent leather camellia stuck on the pink python bag. "Not cool," said La Betty, but she wasn't referring to the strongman's gaze. La Betty was referring to the red boxer trunks, adding, "No price tag no value."

Lowering her gaze La Betty scrolled quickly through:

Grey Saint Laurent Sac de Jour Nano $1,475.
Hermès Blue Saint Cyr Cleménce Evelyne TPM $3,100.

Grey Monogram Vernis Louis Vuitton Alma BB $995.
Micro Fendi Peekaboo $993

Presuming the itsy-bitsy strongman in the window could be intimidated, La Betty insulted him, "You are cheesier than a knock-off." In her most persuasive voice she recited a righteous incantation,

> "The ultimate driving machine
> Melts in your mouth not in your hand
> I'm lovin' it zoom zoom
> It's the real thing snap crackle pop
> Say it with flowers stronger than dirt
> Just do it finger lickin' good."

La Betty's psyche was a treasure house of slogans, jingles and ad copy. La Betty could not stomach phantom troublemakers like this weight lifter, the impudent entities who tempted her away from The Good Life. Whenever she was invaded by hostile ideologies La Betty recited commercial catch phrases, the mantras of consumerism. La Betty had every faith that these would thwart the enemy.

La Betty knew that sooner or later an anti-materialist entity might reappear, often quite vaporous. Predictably the vapour's shape would change, often into something La Betty considered nonsense. There is no grasping intangible visions. Someone other than La Betty might be able to decipher them, if only they didn't change so quickly. Rarely the sound of La Betty's hiss would cause intangible visions to wrinkle and whither like dry autumn leaves; if so La Betty could just pucker her lips and blow; her condo's Febrezified air would be restored, and La Betty would resume her indulgence, for example, reading BagTrends aloud slowly. This time to her satisfaction La Betty detected a potent spell in the BagTrend list:

> Sac de jewel
> Blue Saint *confit*

Peekaboo Plush
993.

Not even this spell could disintegrate the strongman at the window. La Betty glared at him. She scowled. She was very irritated. In a gesture of defiance La Betty reapplied her cobalt blue lipstick.

"Embodiment, flexibility, a centre of gravity," the strongman said. "Weight lifting is a humble praxis."

"Praxis?" La Betty pondered silently. Was *Praxis* a brand name?

Now the wee strongman's face became warmer, as if, after all, it was cookie dough. "Come with me to the Main Street 'Y' and you will discover everything in between your mind and your body."

"Sac de jewel... Blue Saint *confit*... Peekaboo Plush... 993," spoke La Betty with a slight growl in her voice. The bizarre little strongman's invitation held no attraction for La Betty. She emphasized this with a tantrum, pitching a pair of Caroline Groves bespoke Blue Lace Chalcedon high heels at the window.

The half-naked strongman twirled his barbell so swiftly it became a toy propeller. The strongman's tar-black hair responded by tightening, and beside every curl between the swirls, so many pearls as if it was composing a rhyme. The curls formed a cursive script, a French song perhaps, or maybe a Danish recipe. The strongman's eyes turned white as golf balls. "You will regret this," the strongman said.

"I'm not *list*ening," La Betty answered in a childish lilt.

J'adore

La Betty was arranging twelve tiny coins in a straight line on the top of her rare Jacques Hauville mahogany desk. Compared to the luster of the gleaming mahogany the tiny coins looked worn and grimy. They were worn, and nicked at some of the edges, for the coins were 1,850 years old. Each one was a silver denarius minted when Marcus Aurelius Antoninus Augustus was Emperor of the Roman Empire. Each coin was worth USD $1792.56. The coins were not identical, but the Emperor's features were basically unvaried—the short curly hair, the close-cropped beard that narrowed considerably along the jaw line up to the ear, the pointed nose, the narrow moustache, and on some of the coins, bags under his eyes.

La Betty slid her gray wool Baleri Italia Donna chair backwards, slightly away from the desk. She clutched the chill gray arm bars at the sides of the chair. The chair was gangly, its simple metal form and the plain tubular legs gave an insectoid impression; just as, at times, La Betty herself gave an insectoid impression. She was dressed in a priceless wintergreen 1960s Traina linen shift with a broad vermillion border along the bottom hem. La Betty's single bobby pin was a slender zig zag pure silver bar along which twelve petite round-cut emeralds glistened; it could almost be mistaken for a poisonous caterpillar.

La Betty abruptly pulled herself close to the desk and scooped up the coins in her right hand. Holding the coins loosely she shook them. She held her closed fist up to her ear, listening to the coins tapping against each other. She shook them over and over again, listening intently to their faint, chipped clicking. La Betty believed she was hearing the sound of twelve times $1792.56, whatever that added up to, but the jittery clinking was otherwise a meaningless sound; it would never really add up to anything. In and of itself, nevertheless, the infinitesimal clatter of the coins was familiar, comforting, a reassuring tremor that La Betty at first couldn't identify. But only at first: she soon recognized the sound as very much like the shy mutter of the humidifier in her childhood bedroom. La Betty strayed into a trance and let the coins spill onto the desk.

She looked at the disarray of coins as if she was watching them through an airplane window. Some of them were still slightly trembling. Of course some were lying face down, their details indistinct. Sensing the perverse interruption that was occurring La Betty shivered. A deceiving entity was distorting the scene. No doubt the entity would soon be imposing an insipid affirmation of spiritual or social awakening, some idea that had been ignored since 1999. La Betty was startled when the admonition actually slithered off the coin and presented itself as a paragraph of tiny tarnished Scrabble™ tiles. She wished she didn't feel compelled to read the relocated inscription,

> "So you were born to feel 'nice'? Instead of doing things and experiencing them? Don't you see the plants, the birds, the ants and spiders and bees going about their individual tasks, putting the world in order, as best they can? And you're not willing to do your job as a human being?"

La Betty jumped off the chair and stood above the trance. So, the bearded celebrity was advertising the

Aurelius, whatever that was. Whatever that was, and ît wasn't nice, ît was moſtly about bugs. The bearded celebrîty was so awful compared to Matthew McConaughey advertising a Lincoln. La Betty was very quick to pull open one of the desk drawers. She lifted up her small $1857 silver chainmail purse and twiſted open the claſp. She pulled forth from ît her $400 cloud whîte Swiss lace handkerchief. She placed the handkerchief in her lap and gathered up all twelve of the tiny silver coins; they were dropped briskly into her purse.

La Betty locked the dainty purse. She shut ît into the drawer. She ſtepped back, haughtily fluttering the handkerchief above her head, inhaling wîth élan. "And now ît's the time…" La Betty proclaimed the exact words of an ad for a favourîte perfume. In the ad a seemingly nude Charlize Theron is slîthering like an amphibian through shallow pools of ǵilded liquid. "The only way out is up," La Betty continued, "It's not to Heaven. It's to a new you." La Betty inhaled deeply as the brilliant scent filled the air. "The future is gold. *J'adore* Dior. The future is gold. *J'adore* Dior."

Snowy Lane

An Austrian Philosopher walked along a laneway between Victorian mansions on one side and on the other side withered cabbage gardens of the working poor. The philosopher's specialty was not political theory. To him the scene was neutral. The simple lane was straight and it was narrow. He had always felt comforted by dusk, when indistinct colours become shadows and streetlamps are like cats' eyes. It was pleasant to perceive this quiet lane as an illustration of his state of mind.

The philosopher was contemplating symbolization. For this he decided to observe the back alley as an ordinary place devoid of theatrical moments, a place neither of movements nor of sound. Beneath a fresh but unimpressive snowfall the roofs were unified visually by their toppings of flat white. The philosopher felt he could accept this visual motif, but otherwise he insisted to himself that the laneway was "blank." Toying with the vernacular the philosopher described the scene to himself as "empty," a word that betrayed a conceptual difficulty the philosopher was confronting.

The philosopher hoped that he was walking where the pure idea of symbol would not be disturbed. For quite some time he had been considering the idea of symbol as simply that, pure idea. He wanted to eliminate if he could the certainty that symbol as pure idea is oxymoronic; he wanted to propose a symbol of nothing, not a symbol in the sense that words and numbers symbolize. "Nothing," "void," "vacant" were commonplaces and vernacular, insufficient for philosophic inquiry. Zero is after all a word when it isn't arithmetical.

In this nondescript alley it seemed there would be no object so unusual as to have a symbolic effect. The alley was quintessentially austere. The philosopher wanted his thoughts to be quintessentially austere. In such a place the contradiction he was trying to dissolve could yield to innovative reasoning. The philosopher did expect an interruption by a crow plunging into view, but he would deny that every single crow is by definition symbolic.

The philosopher was cogitating the possible existence of a symbol for nothing, a symbol of nothing. The philosopher was conducting a mind experiment in which a visual symbol of nothing was attainable, beyond reduction to a practical word like "vacuum" or "abyss." The contradiction was whether a recognizable something, a single visual something could always and instantly evoke the idea of nothing.

La Betty, unfettered by abstractions, slept through most of this particular dream. Until the very end of this dream it had appeared to be only a scene of an ordinary man walking down an ordinary laneway. After all, the quiet little philosopher's thought was invisible.

This philosopher was, however, a ruse. La Betty's dream was being invaded by an entity in the guise of a philosopher. The entity in disguise as an abstract thinker was using stillness to lull La Betty away from her lifestyle. Numerous strategies had already failed, but there was always another miscreant with another appalling idea. This entity's challenge was to manipulate La Betty into mistaking her blunt superficiality for abstract thought.

The appeal of abstract thought can be its self-referential logic. Numbers are the starkest example of this, the way numbers procreate, subtract each other, pile up and on many occasions disengage themselves from common sense, measuring, tracking and predicting events about other numbers. The faux-philosopher of course was not planning to explain this to La Betty. This entity's bold strategy was to sneak abstraction in where La Betty's utterly shallow attitude prevailed, to insert abstraction where La Betty had established superficiality (In a sense La Betty's superficiality and her dedication to image have a self-referential logic.) The philosopher-fiend had taken on the challenge of swooping La Betty into the world of ideas, propositions and dialectical reasoning.

La Betty began experiencing the philosopher-phantasm's solemnity as if it was a cloud of gnats. She woke herself up with her own slapping and flailing. La Betty immediately recognized the invasion of the dream for what it was. To assume that pure surface-adoration could be replaced by unadorned abstract thinking couldn't have been sillier. La Betty looked around her sitting room, at the bare Tiffany blue walls, the Swarovski transparent crystal chandelier, the porcelain sculpture of Michael Jackson with a chimpanzee, and beneath it the Iranian Kashkoli Gabbeh rug, the green lacquered surface of the vacant walk-in closet. The look of all these deluxe objects soothed La Betty. She sighed and she luxuriated in ownership.

Ishtar

La Betty perceived a scuffling sound just outside her condo front door. No one could have secretly ascended by the elevator unless its security bell was broken. Yet without taking the elevator, no one would have means to reach La Betty's threshold. La Betty opened her front door judiciously, just enough for a slender sightline.

La Betty spied a small ornate gift box near the elevator. The box shone like ruby, its glassy colour deep and unsullied. La Betty assumed the dramatic symbol on the lid of the box was a classy trademark. The symbol was embossed on a gold disk attached to the crimson lid. The symbol was an eight-point star, the bases of each point joined to a ruby red central circle. The eight-point star itself was late sunset blue.

La Betty's entire consciousness was fixated on the dazzling box. To La Betty a gleaming tidy box could only mean there was a brilliant object inside. Her antique green silk Fortuny dressing gown fluttered as she sashayed toward the enticing object on the polished ebony floor. When she lifted the box it released a hazy aroma, an intermingling of grass, licorice and dry martini with a twist of lemon. La Betty took a deep breath and tiptoed back to the east loggia of her condo. She lowered herself onto the juniper green seat of her $12,559.38 Otto Wagner armchair. Sitting there always imbued La Betty with the self-assurance only money can buy.

La Betty was very pleased to lift the lid of the box. It was surprisingly hefty. Inside, a perfect dome of white kaolinite clay was nestled in a wrapper of citrus green chiffon. La Betty grabbed the swaddled clay dome and peeled away the organza. The white clay was surprisingly warm, surprisingly soft. La Betty was compelled to take it in her right hand and squeeze forcefully. La Betty laid this altered clod on the deep red glass surface of the nearby Osvaldo Borsani table. The substance seemed to solidify. She then noticed there was a tiny scroll in the box. It must have been under the organza at the bottom. La Betty pinched the scroll between thumb and forefinger and then glanced back toward the squeezed kaolinite. It had stiffened vaguely in the form of a seated figure, a monkey in pleated pantaloons wearing a pointed hat with eight spikes. A barbed choker was quite prominent around the neck and from it hung an eight-point star. This simian idol sported impressive falcon wings. All these features looked like they had been eroded in a sandstorm.

La Betty loosened the scroll's slender ochre binding. When La Betty dropped the binding on the table top the filament immediately coiled like a garden horsehair worm. Distracted by the bold, unusual, indeed medieval rubric at the top of the scroll La Betty assumed she was about to read a slogan tailored to elite consumers. Accordingly she recited the slogan for LuxorEye lapis lazuli-dusted mascara. "Eye it - try it - buy it!"

The scroll was read aloud, but not by La Betty. She glanced quickly at the monkey idol but its lips weren't moving. The only other mouth in the room was that of the garden horsehair worm. La Betty knew perverse interruption was taking place once again by phantasms antagonistic toward La Betty's devotion to Spectacle. The garden horsehair worm with a voice like Leonard Cohen was reading aloud, "History is our Mother.

Honour her in all your days." La Betty went on the attack.

"You are more. Take away the risk and you can do anything!"

This had been the slogan for LuxorEye nonsmear midnightsheen mascara. La Betty conflated the risk of smeared mascara with the risk of granting credibility to these pushy phantasms trying to change her life. She was aghast at the impudence of these pious messengers with no understanding of the twenty-first century. The garden horsehair worm continued, "Such a man was Herodotus who honoured our Mother in all his days."

The clay Ishtar monkey straightened his eight-point star pendant and quoted Herodotus,

> He is the best man who,
> when making his plans, fears
> and reflects on everything
> that can happen to him, but
> in the moment of action
> is bold.

La Betty swooped up the monkey and used it to hammer the garden horsetail worm. "A Taste of the Truth!" La Betty proclaimed this, "A Taste of the Truth," the slogan for White Luxe Glamourous White Whitening Fresh Mint Flavour Mouthwash.

Green Man

At midnight while La Betty dozed rain began to fall. La Betty's slumber had been restless, perhaps because of the bubbles in the after-dinner Danziger Goldwasser paired with a gold-polka-dot chocolate truffle. On the edge of sleep La Betty heard the rain, and then mistook the raindrops on the window for Danziger Goldwasser bubbles. The bubbles were captivating. The bubbles glistened like little spheres of rainbow. They slid like tiny pools of pure mercury.

La Betty began sleepwalking. She left her bed and padded across her pricey Iranian Kashkoli Gabbeh rug. Moving as gracefully as a glider La Betty sidestepped the silk bonsai acacia tree atop her Osvaldo Borsani table. She stopped at the bedroom window without colliding into anything. La Betty marveled as the raindrops turned paper-white. They coalesced in sheets as they slid toward the bottom of the window. Most of them had a strange purple bubble in the middle. The raindrops seemed to be coagulating, and the purple bubbles organizing themselves as if they were forming strictly patterned lace. Then, as with a long fine-tooth comb, the coalescing droplets were plowed top to bottom. The paths of the comb's teeth created narrow grass-green furrows. As La Betty dreamed she was witnessing all this, she began to walk backwards, not toward her bed but in a direction perpendicular to her bed. She drifted backwards along a line that intersected no objects or

furniture. When La Betty reached a wall she woke up
and opened her eyes. She expected to be in bed. The
view before her was momentarily disorienting until she
beheld the window's conspicuous melding raindrops
and the slender green lines.

This concatenation of droplets, bubbles, green filaments
and the formless night behind them was not amorphous.
La Betty clearly discerned that from her distance the
window framed an actual figure: a man with a serious
face possibly dressed in a white lab coat with three
pens in his left front pocket. He was focusing as if on a
specimen, but the windowsill cut off the view.

Not looking up, neither moving nor moving his lips, the
man was speaking. His voice was strained and saddened.
He seemed to be pleading for someone to openly
embrace and act upon his words.

> "If we pollute the air, water and soil that keep us
> alive and well, and destroy the biodiversity that
> allows natural systems to function, no amount
> of money will save us. No amount of money. If
> we pollute and destroy no amount of money
> will save us."[*]

"Perfectly balanced with no bubbles added!"

La Betty had always considered this slogan to be
quite charming. It suited the present situation well
enough, and La Betty felt smug about her allusion to
both Goldwasser and the weather. She offered this
slogan, as she so often did, to ward off interference and
temptation by pious ghosts undead since the twentieth
century. This particular entity was especially outré.
Everyone that La Betty currently sees on television or
the Internet has long since lost loyalty to Planet Earth.
They claim that shameless corporations have become

---

[*] Liberally modified from David Suzuki.

faceless feudal lords. The borders of financial territories are static, no need for enforcing by what was formerly known as international law. Nouvelle courtiers enjoy the delusion that technicians will fix the planet before all the great-great grandchildren are doomed. Nouvelle peasants, exhausted by environmentalism, have lost enthusiasm for any activity that would result in great-great grandchildren.

La Betty knew at once this portrait beseeching her to conservation was completely out of step with the late twenty-first century. This Green Man had to be a perverse interruption. His voice had to be the voice of an untrustworthy, offensive tempter. This unfashionable fiend was defying La Betty's ideals. To proclaim her values (the value of extreme wealth, the value of buying power, the value of materialism) La Betty insisted, "Perfectly balanced with no bubbles added! No bubbles added! No bubbles added!" She stepped forward readily to prove to the fiend she was unmoved.

As La Betty returned to the window, she began to chant soft advice to the sham environmentalist. "Waterproof your face," she chanted. This "Endless Summer" make up ad countered the rain-drippy man's admonition. "Waterproof your face!" La Betty shouted. The forlorn watery figure tried to turn his back but instead abruptly dissolved. The raindrops and midnight were formless now. La Betty stood close to the window staring past the transparent rain, toward English Bay. She was already imagining magnificent ships on the waters, magnificent ships bringing exorbitant treasures inland.

Shikaakwa

La Betty looked up into her $1,080 antique Italian mirror. The diameter of the brass mirror frame was forty centimeters, a perfect circle with six dainty round bolt heads symmetrically placed. In its simplicity it resembled an overturned hubcap. Around the outer edge of the frame, like a corona of shiny buckshot, metal beading caught the light as it ricocheted round and round in iridescent olive, Guinness beer brown and amber with beams of gold.

The mirror was attached to La Betty's bedroom wall at such a height, and at such a precise angle, that it would reflect many of the taller and higher objects in the room but never reflect La Betty's face. La Betty delighted in the images of her possessions as if they were being mysteriously broadcast from a magical planet or fairyland.

La Betty was sitting comfortably on the white $13,699.99 Icelandic Eiderdown comforter that embraced her bed. As she lounged the $1,226 Dolce & Gabbana oat-coloured Boucle Shift she wore followed but did not constrict the contours of La Betty's skinny form. La Betty had been looking up at the mirror to enjoy the reflection of the ancient fabric handiwork she had just acquired from the estate of Brigadier General William "Billy" Mitchell. La Betty had been attracted to its beauty and its astronomical price. Beauty and breath-taking price confirmed, La Betty knew what she liked. It was her mistaken opinion that this artifact was a ladies' handbag. Starting with "bandolier," La Betty hadn't understood some of the words in the auction house's description of this venerable object. The word *aazhooningwa'igan* frightened and annoyed her.

> The bandolier bag, or more properly the *aazhooningwa'igan*, features red loop-weave cotton-tape piping and white beaded edging. The bag is fully loom-beaded on a solid white background with large pink stylized garlic shapes outlined in black, and small leaves, pink and red without borders, and even smaller black leaves with triangular yellow centers. The horizontal same-size rectangle sewn to the top of the bag is spot stitched onto a black backing in an asymmetrical floral design of a crooked twig coiling around a bulbous pink corm, a blue seed pod and a variety of bright green leaf types. Along the lower edge of the bag, ending in red wool tassels, traditional symbols in blue, pink, black and yellow beading adorn eight wide tabs.

La Betty had glanced at this description. She knew what the word *garlic* meant, of course, but had assumed it was a typo, the actual word undoubtedly being *gardenia*. Easily distracted by all the names of pretty colours La Betty hadn't thought it worthwhile to read the description carefully. She did spot another typo—*corm*, easily correcting it to *corn*. La Betty's eyelids fluttered and then she looked up at her mirror; the glass disk was shimmering darkly, displaying the face of the Man in the Moon. He was exactly as he looks in the sky, with a complexion like smoky quartz.

Emerging from the mirror, the moon head was attached to a body, a middle aged, chunky male body. He grasped the mirror's edge, hung there for a moment, and then, letting go, falling, he kept his balance as he landed on both feet. When landed, he was 5 ft 10 inches tall. La Betty recognized the brand of his faded camo pants, $150 pret-a-porter from Cabela's. The sneakers were generic. She couldn't imagine what brand of long-sleeved gray hoodie he was wearing. But La Betty recognized his bandolier shoulder bag, "*My* bag!" she thought. She understood, nevertheless, that this man was an annoying phantom. Another perverse interruption, a figment armed with twentieth century adages that had become totally outré by 1999.

The man reached into the a*azhooningwa'igan*. With one hand he had retrieved pink corms. In the other, dangling by green shoots, swayed a bunch of small, putrescent white garlic bulbs. He took a step toward La Betty, as if he was offering La Betty the reeking white bulbs. La Betty stared, aghast at the odor. He said gently, "This vegetable, this *shikaakwa*, knows more than you do."

La Betty swirled, turned her back on the phantom and walked stiffly toward her $11,990 Louis XVI little white dresser. La Betty fussed, "I know where the *Gardenia* is," and recited the ad copy for *Gardenia*, Frédéric Malle's $1,265 Eau de Parfum,

> "Fifty ml of natural oud,
> gardenia petal's
> magnificent texture,
> refreshing opening of
> pink pepper. Laudanum
> and vibrant frankincense;
> extra warmth of oak moss
> completes a very dark focal point."

Prince and Princess

La Betty was thrilled to read the description of a royal commemorative platter. The portrait of the prince and princess beguiled La Betty into a swoon. The enchanting illustration was well detailed, as one would expect from a magazine that cost one hundred dollars. The illustration revived memories of all the glamorous photographs that had captivated La Betty over the years. The portraits on the plate were shining just as the prince and princess shone together when the two of them had believed in their romance. The princess was radiantly beautiful, or perhaps radiantly photogenic, but flat glossy photos were just what La Betty preferred. The platter pictured early days when the prince's hair was thick and dark, short of course, befitting a navy officer. The prince wore a dark, rather too ample suit, a white shirt and a droopy black bow tie. The prince was lanky and his posture was well balanced, unlike his aging father, a consort who'd spent his entire life leaning forward at the waist with his hands clasped behind his back.

The princess was wearing a long white raw silk gown. The formfitting bodice was of the same fabric yet with the faintest tinge of rose, leaving ample room above the bosom for a delicate gold chain graced by three little emeralds and twenty-four tiny pearls. The long white sleeves were the same material as the skirt, embroidered with miniscule yellow roses and hundreds of over-sized pink thorns. The ad copy alongside the picture included guarantees that the background—the bottom of the commemorative platter—was cream white enhanced by a fine-lined gold grid.

The closer La Betty looked, however, the more incongruous the image and the advertising copy became. Inexplicably the text failed to mention a prominent silver inscription that encircled the plate's Prussian blue border:

> REX VIR BONUS HABEAT BONAM
> IN HUNC MODUM CANIS.
> [A good king is as loyal as a good dog.]

La Betty couldn't remember ever seeing a photograph of the prince with such a ruddy complexion. His nose, as was traditional in the royal family, looked very narrow, long and pointed but here it was reddish brown, and the flared nostrils surprisingly large. La Betty held the magazine at different angles to check whether it was the lighting in her condo's reading room that accounted for the colour of the prince's huge round eyes. The eyes were as orange as pumpkins. La Betty was offended that the prince had let his fingernails grow too long. The nails were bone white and slightly curled back toward the palm. Now La Betty became wary of the princess' image. She expected travesty.

The head of the princess was set askew and strangely dissociated from the foreground. Her hair was bushy and gray with pink highlights. The eyes were round and perverse, like pools of butterscotch pudding.

It was happening once again, this time within the lavish magazine page. La Betty's solitude was being infiltrated by malevolent spirits. La Betty's leisure was being invaded by nefarious fiends. These phantasms were rearranging the perspective. These nasty twentieth century apparitions intended to obstruct La Betty's absorption into *Century of the Spectacle* magazine.

La Betty heard a whispering sound, like pages turning. The rapidly swishing pages were like voices on the wind, "You have many toys but you never play. Most of your toys do nothing. Let us move in. You needn't ever shop again."

La Betty quickly fortified her disdain with a slogan, "Stop Time. Stay Young. Stop Time. Stay Young." She also intoned the product's name "24-carat gold, royal jelly Crème Imperial moisturizer," and glanced again at the platter. The figure labeled "prince" and the pinkish-gray one labeled "princess" were Spaniels.

La Betty stood up straight. She thrust the magazine against her reading room's ammonite gray enameled-lava floor. She kicked away her baby harp seal fur slippers and reached for a nearby pitcher of Danziger Goldwasser. She doused the magazine fiercely, and then marched boldly toward her prized $5,897 Dutch Wim Rietveld Enameled 1960s bookcase. La Betty reached for a prominent leather-bound sheaf of paper. This odd artist's book was hexagonal and the russet leather had been stained to look like wood. Still indignant, La Betty snatched out one of the loose-leaf pages. La Betty stood there loudly reading,

> All the world's a shop,
> And we are but customers in it.
> We have our entrances and exits;
> The best of us have many styles
> and money enough to obey our fancies.

Fedora

La Betty sank gracefully into her George Nelson black leather 1953 "Coconut" chair. While her swinging feet kicked lightly her hand hastily swiped one past another 20th century Caroline Reboux hat image on her iPad. Unexpectedly a man's confident voice became audible,

"Our hats will be made in velvet, straw, cork, light metals, glass, celluloid, particle board, leather, sponge, fiber, neon tubes, etc.... There will be nothing in common between the servility of tour guides and the proud inventive originality of the fascist Futurists of today!"

La Betty glanced at the iPad. Nothing had changed. The pitch of the confident voice varied with La Betty's swipe tempo, measured, then manic. The contrast between the man's declaration and Reboux millinery was extreme.

Suddenly, simultaneously, voice and image halted at a fashionable dark fedora. This $891 fedora was no longer available at any store in New York, Paris or Milano.

"One hundred per cent rabbit fur felt fedora hat, in midnight blue, with tonal grosgrain hatband featuring brass logo hardware. The front crease is pinched. The lining is 60% viscose, 40% cotton. Made in Italy. More

smiling, less worrying! Life is not about waiting for the storm to pass but learning to dance in the rain!"
La Betty was extremely annoyed—but not surprised. La Betty felt disdain for disaster-prone sentiments of the twentieth century, all of them, from aggressively foolish to inanely useless, in this instance from puerile Futurists to the plethora of 20th century self-help advice. And, tastelessly saccharine, the latter platitudes were inked in gold lettering on the Fedora's tonal grosgrain.

These sappy gold sentences could only be insertions by perverse entities. Once again La Betty was being assailed by obnoxious phantoms; the entities often, as again this time, spoke with exuberant snarls, like the television voice-over in a 2016 Ford-150 truck commercial. Once again La Betty was being needled to convert, this time to a nice lady who makes it her business to bestow cheer.

La Betty rushed to the window. She couldn't discern English Bay through the low-lying clouds smudging the glass. She stared at the formless smear that had obscured the outside world. La Betty was soothed by this withered veil. It matched her indifference to bodily desire. Indifference was the ashen background against which La Betty's superficiality glittered.

She cautiously looked again at the iPad, let the Futurist voice resume. The fedora had slid away in silence. The Fine Paints of Europe website had replaced it, offering "dead flat, oil-based interior colours of gray mist, winter sky, silverblade, North Sea and storm cloud."

The window's obscured view was not dead flat, for as La Betty gazed thoughtlessly the fog thickened and spun. A form seemed to be condensing, revolving like a whirlpool, stopping abruptly to become a hat, a 1955 Jeanne Lanvin hat designed by Antonio del Castillo. La Betty recognized it. She had always admired this hat, but under present circumstances a very uncomfortable ambivalence emerged. The image of the magnificent hat thrilled La Betty, who had memorized every pleat and fold of its divine velvet convolutions. The hat was an enchanted object, not quite as symmetrical as a bird's nest, not quite animated as a twirling clump of seaweed. No, La Betty adored the hat because it was inorganic, a paradox of vulnerable soft rigidity. Meddling entities, however, were conjuring the hazy haute couture headpiece. No doubt it was their intention to illustrate that all of La Betty's fascinations were amoral, and she resented the tone.

To her horror, the hat undulated into the shape of a mouth, speaking in a quiet whiny voice. La Betty heard,

"A smile is the light in your window that tells others that there is a caring, sharing person inside.

Remember even though the outside world might be raining, if you keep on smiling the sun will soon show its face and smile back at you.

With Mother Teresa's words I remind you, 'We shall never know all the good that a simple smile can do.'"

La Betty whirled away from the window. She luxuriated in the swish of her silk day dress: a Madame Vionnet version of St. Gabriel's salmon-coloured tunic in the illuminated manuscript of the hymn "Drop down dew, you heavens from above…." La Betty flung the iPad into the Coconut chair and chanted,

> Chanel's casino
> John Galliano's marble steps
> Maison Martin Margiela's bejewelled masks
> Iris Van Herpen's *cymatic*
> Valentino's red dresses
> Viktor & Rolf: catwalk for enormous bobbleheads

Unabridged

The 1937 *Webster's Unabridged Dictionary* had been set on the highest shelf of La Betty's Wim Rietveld Enameled 1960s bookcase. The $500 *Respoke* Fabia floral printed silk espadrilles La Betty wore couldn't raise her to the top shelf, and La Betty had never owned a pair of high heels. She deemed high heel shoes too gregarious—unnerving for a solitary woman such as herself. La Betty had dragged her "Cappuccino Foam"-tinted calfskin footstool out of the bedroom and into the library. With remarkable equilibrium La Betty had stepped up and stood on the footstool. She hadn't worried about the soles of her espadrilles smudging the calfskin, because soles of La Betty's footwear had never touched any surface outside of her immaculate condo.

The dictionary was a massive book, but La Betty had managed to lower it. She set it on the polished block of petrified wood that capped her minimalist end table. Between pages 1009 and 1010 she discovered a hanky. La Betty slid the hanky out from the dictionary. Each of its four sides was contoured by five scalloped edges. And near each mauve scallop edge was a nosegay of four five-petal royal purple flowers with bright yellow centres. Under each of these small bouquets were five serrated oblong leaves. Under these malachite-green leaves were pale pink doilies, also scalloped, and pierced by six malachite-green stems, bound by a long royal purple ribbon. All this presented an imaginary, vibrant garden speckled with fifty-four scattered purple buds and fifty-four itty-bitty pink five-petal rosettes with hollow centres. There was more to see, but this complex of shapes and colours vibrated noisily in La Betty's brain.

La Betty placed the hanky on the petrified wood and looked again at the open dictionary. Between page 1009 and 1010 she noticed an unnumbered page of weakly tinted flowers. The flowers were numbered 1-12, their numbers and names in tiny print at the bottom of the page. These were the names of common flowers most people recognize: African violet, carnation, daffodil, dandelion, gardenia, gladiola, hollyhock, lily of the valley, orchid, pansy, rose, tulip. La Betty felt bored as her eyes meandered over this uninspired floral array. She was wishing to see illustrations of terribly expensive rarely-gathered blossoms, like the *Shenzhen Nongke*, the Juliet rose, the *Kadupul*, the saffron crocus, and the *Gold of Kinabalu* orchid.

On page 1010 the word "gardener," was defined and its etymology reviewed. This included the Old English word wyrtweard, literally "plant-guard." There was an unusual woodcut illustration of tree stumps and a wyrtweard in simple garb, a red tunic tied around the waist with leather cord, tight dark blue leggings, knee-high woolen socks and crude leather footwear. The wyrtweard appeared to be a woman.

This illustration was quite small, though it filled a disproportionate amount of space for a dictionary picture. As La Betty glanced at the wyrtweard woman's hat she perceived that it wasn't a hat. It was shoulder-length brown hair with blond highlights. La Betty immediately recognized the tunic. It wasn't a tunic. It was a $1330 red plaid Pierre Balmain shirt. La Betty abruptly leaned backwards and scowled. It seemed the wyrtweard was scowling too, though her eyes and brow were dim behind chunky $250 Dolce and Gabbana tortoiseshell sunglasses. The wyrtweard's shoes were

$800 Converse sneakers. La Betty focused on the flat painted face; without hesitation she recognized the wyrtweard: Melania Trump. Melania had turned her back away from a short Medieval wyrtweard dressed in a red tunic tied around his waist with leather cord, tight dark blue leggings, knee-high woolen socks and crude leather footwear.

Vertically from top to bottom along the left side of this woodcut, printed in anachronistic *Courier* typeface La Betty read what Melania was supposedly thinking:

```
"There is no gardening without humility,
"The flower that smells the sweetest is shy and lowly;
"Gardening is an instrument of grace,
"Always remember the beauty of the garden, for
  — is peace.
Those flowers on your hanky are Deadly Nightshade."
```

La Betty aggressively shut the thirteen pound book. It sounded like the door of a Lexus had been slammed. La Betty was infuriated by this wyrtweard's 20th century sentimentality and horticultural sarcasm.

Vehemently, to dissipate any influence from the phantom's sappy aroma, La Betty shouted the names of costly floral perfumes,

> "Paco Rabane *Lady Million*
> YSL *Blossom Supérieur*
> Jimmy Choo *Blossom*
> Gucci *Bloom*
> Dior *Blooming Bouquet*
> Moschino *Pink Bouquet*
> Prada *Infusion d'Iris*
> Bvlgari *Splendida Iris d'Or*
> Michael Kors *Glam Jasmine*
> Givenchy *Dahlia Divin*
> Elie Saab *Rose Couture*
> Escada *Cherry in the Air*."

Feu d'artifice

La Betty sat staring out the thirtieth-floor window of her condo overlooking English Bay. A stupendous fireworks display had been scheduled for 11 PM. La Betty glanced often at her $4,720 Gucci gold and malachite *Signoria* wristwatch. La Betty enjoyed waiting. She felt exceptional each time she focussed on the lustrous malachite face of the excessively swank *Signoria*. La Betty savoured the lively interplay of the opulent bracelet gold and the pure inscrutable green. La Betty had been informed by her jeweler that as early as 4,000 B.C.E. malachite was treasured for its power to protect its wearer from evil spirits. La Betty had sneered at this protection myth, considering all the perverse interruptions she endured, the countless phantasms and wraiths with their utterly misplaced zeal. A parade of clueless 20th century spirits had been pressuring La Betty to abandon her superficial lifestyle, their interventions having persisted for years.

A fireworks barge was bobbing safely on the westernmost periphery of the bay. Not far from shore a master of ceremonies and a group of hip hop dancers were posed on a well-lit floating platform. The MC's commentary, alternating with music, was to be broadcast and streamed to all citizens who were nowhere near English Bay. La Betty was indifferent to the cause of the celebration: Worldwide Marvel in Motion Bicycles Are Better Day. The publicity for this event had emphasized the choreography theme "Dancing with Bicycles."

The promotion on the Marvel in Motion website had quoted Jane Jacobs' warning, "Traffic arteries, along with parking lots, gas stations, and drive-ins are powerful and insistent instruments of city destruction." There was no mistaking the logos of the official aluminum siding, official pest control and official house paint of Marvel in Motion. The last word was left to Mike Burrows' futuristic claim. Mike Burrows, winner of the 1992 Barcelona Olympics 4000-meter bicycle race, had promised, "The bicycle is the one piece of sports equipment that can save the planet."

The English Bay extravaganza began with a succession of Roman Candles. Next, the big surprise: a structure had been mounted in the dark, away from shore and far from the main fireworks barge; from it, suddenly, hundreds of sizzling red and white flashes displayed a colossal blazing bicycle. Tethered little red and white rockets produced the illusion that the bicycle wheels were turning. When the bike image gradually fizzled and blackened the MC proclaimed, "Yes, folks, this bicycle is totally burnt out, but the future for bicycle culture is BRIGHT."

The dancing began to the sound of Notorious B.I.G.'s "Born Again." Those two words, *born again*, infuriated and offended La Betty. Those words epitomized the preaching of the phantoms, who were forever underestimating La Betty's autonomy. The very thought of yet another impending visitation prompted La Betty to shout, "Happy, happy fashion. There is not much more to it than that!" So comforting was this Marc Jacobs proclamation La Betty asserted it again, "Happy, happy fashion. There is not much more to it than that!"

La Betty looked closely at the next barrage of fireworks. There were three prodigious pink "wave" explosions, and La Betty was sure they were rolling directly toward her window. This could only mean that a phantasm was close by. "Body Wave™ perms cascade in beachy waves, giving hair more staying power!" La Betty declared as she frowned at the surge of rosy ripples.

"And now," the MC announced, "the fireworks song by Pink! She may not be here in Vancouver tonight but play the song and fire the rockets! You are so-o-o right on, Pink. 'Glitter in the Air!'" Reluctantly La Betty conceded that, with the window closed and all of her devices turned off, hearing the MC's babbling was obviously preternatural.

La Betty watched an eruption of fiery glitter descending from the sky. At first the embers glowed red, then maroon, and then, as they multiplied by the thousands, La Betty recognized their colour as MILK™ Supernova holographic hyper-lavender eye shadow.

After the glitter shower The MC forsook all pretension of being human, expounding the supreme assets of the bicycle in a voice that implied the bicycle had just arrived from Jupiter, "It takes less energy to bicycle one mile than it takes to walk one mile," he squeaked, "One hundred calories can power a cyclist for three miles, but it would only power a car 280 feet!"

La Betty frowned, stamped her foot and recited,

> "Take your hair to paradise.
> Happy hair, happy you.
> Love is Purpelle™ dry shampoo!"

Under the Chandelier

The peau de soie white satin Celebrity Wedding Money Bag had been delivered erroneously to La Betty's condo. When La Betty had opened the fire-ant-red box the gleaming bag was nestled in many ruffles of silver-splinter tissue paper. La Betty recoiled from the money bag; it resembled a fresh diaper. It provoked her girlhood nightmare of a swimming bag of living skin. Gingerly between her thumb and forefinger she flipped it onto the floor. She fished out the tissue paper and flattened it on the top of her $1221 solid iron silver-leafed Chaouen pedestal table. Unlike the elegant ashen little table, the tissue paper shone like fireflies, reflecting the iridescent light of the chandelier overhead.

The chandelier was an exact copy of one of the chandeliers in Coco Chanel's suite at the Paris Ritz Hotel. The tissue mirrored it well at first, but as La Betty's forefinger traced the iconic details the reflection of teardrop crystals began to bloat.

La Betty gasped as one of the bloated crystal teardrops continued expanding until its surface revealed grooves. And so La Betty anticipated another uncanny interruption. Soon an abnormal entity would assail her with appalling sentiments.

The widening grooves appeared to be strands of letters:

Nomen mihi est Providentiae. Lucius Annaeus Seneca dixit ad me audivi, Aliis bona falsa circumdedi et animos inanes velut long fallacique somnio lusi. Auro illos et argento et eborer adornavi, intus nihil est.*

La Betty closed her eyes and looked again. This mumbo-jumbo was actually inscribed on the silver-splinter wrapping paper, its appearance on the swollen crystals an uncanny illusion. La Betty quickly lifted the wrapping paper from the table and onto her lap. La Betty was wearing a copy of the sapphire blue Fortuny "Delphos" tunic Peggy Guggenheim wore in Venice in 1952. The wrapping warped slightly on the soft pleats of the ankle-length dress. La Betty braced herself for an unwelcome, eerie incident.

As she focused more closely on the wrapping, the silver splinters shifted and slid till they formed a rough sketch of a gentleman with a carefully trimmed white beard. He was wearing pale fawn linen trousers and a myrtle green Harris tweed jacket. He was sitting in a 1928 wood and French Beige leather armchair. In his lap was an open book, *Oxford Classical Texts: L. Annaei Senecae*. Improbably this gentleman was murmuring, reading with his lips moving and his forefinger touching each word in sequence. La Betty decided to loathe whatever he was translating.

The gentleman's stentorian voice could evoke anyone's curiosity, but never La Betty's. Yet even with her hands over her ears she could hear, "I am a scholar of the Classics. The current culture disgusts me. As with Horace, '*Odi profanum vulgus.*'—I despise the vulgar rabble." La Betty knew perfectly well that Horace was actually paraphrasing Christian Lacroix, "I never loved the world around me as it was." La Betty wished the scholar might at least be sitting in the voluptuous Christian Lacroix black and blue striped armchair, an allusion to the black and red gowns he had created for Schiaparelli in the autumn of 2013.

The Classics scholar's voice switched ever so slightly toward a patronizing tone, "My dear, *'Miserum te iudico, quod numquam fuisti miser'*—I account you unfortunate because you have never been unfortunate. It's too late for misfortune now, young lady. But it's not too late to learn to read Latin. Join me deciphering the ineffable wisdom! Look at the Frontispiece, supposing you are pictured there; imagine your warm palm upon a cold marble likeness of Seneca's massive head. Run your forefinger along his marble mouth, the font of Stoic virtue. It's not too late!"

La Betty crinkled the silver-splinter wrapping paper in her fist. She tossed it over her shoulder. She stood up, leaned over and set her warm left hand on the cool Chaouen table top. The fingers of her right hand rubbed her pouting crimson mouth. "*For glamour, Ultra Diamond Energy Lips,*" she intoned, "*Ultra Diamond. Ultra Diamond Energy Lips. Energy Lips!*"

---

* "My name is Providence." Lucius Annaeus Seneca heard me say, "I have surrounded others with spurious goods, beguiling their empty minds, as it were, with a long, illusory dream. I have adorned them with gold and silver and ivory, but there is nothing inside them."

JEANNE RANDOLPH

A NOTE ON THE TYPE

The text of this book is set in Mrs Eaves, originally designed by Zuzana Licko in 1996 for the digital type foundry Emigre. It was styled after Baskerville, the famous transitional serif typeface designed in 1757 by John Baskerville. Mrs Eaves was named after Baskerville's live in housekeeper, Sarah Eaves, whom he later married. It features a low x-height contributing to the lightness of the page and an extensive set of unconventional ligatures. Notes are set in its companion sans-serif typeface Mr Eaves, designed by Licko in 2009.

Titles are set in Grand Slang, designed by Nikolas Wrobel in 2019. Its design boldy reinterprets the essence of mid-20th century American calligraphy for contemporary times.

ACKNOWLEDGEMENTS

In a fit of generosity Anthony Kiendl had invited me to choose sixteen works from the vaults of the MacKenzie Art Gallery for a ficto-criticism solo exhibition in 2017. I had chosen artworks most likely to evoke chapters for *My Claustrophobic Happiness*.

I am indebted to Jenifer Papararo, whose happy insight led to six more chapters, this time corresponding to artworks kindly loaned from Plug-In ICA, the University of Winnipeg and the Winnipeg Art Gallery. A second version of *My Claustrophobic Happiness* was installed in the group exhibition, *Days of Reading: Beyond this State of Affairs*.

And then Irene Bindi inspired me to write even more chapters. A naturally sensitive, meticulous and intelligent editor, Irene is everything good as a reader and as an instigator of artful thought.

Kevin Yuen Kit Lo's cover design is hilariously apt. I'm so pleased.

A thousand thanks to ARP.